# Package From The Past

By

Jacqueline Opresnik

ISBN e-book 978-0-9878063-4-5
ISBN soft cover book 978-0-9878063-3-8

This novel is a work of fiction. The names, characters and incidents portrayed in it are the work of the author's imagination. Any resemblance to actual persons, living or dead, is entirely coincidental.

For my best friend and husband Frank.
Years ago we searched together for a man whose name was on a ‘letter from the past’.

# Chapter 1

It was a cool misty morning, a common summer morning in southern Scotland. Young Alexander Cheyne looked out over the lawns of Cheyne Manor, while waiting for the party he had just dialed to answer, and noticed one of the gardeners tidying up the courtyard flower beds. There was a large fountain in the centre of the lawn that draped splatters of water drops evenly over the scalloped edge into a larger bowl beneath it. Alexander's dog, a large Airedale named Bruce splashed the pooling water with his front paws then scampered playfully across the grass dodging back and forth as if seeking attention from the gardener. The phone rang three times then was answered. "Have you made any progress yet?" he inquired.

"Not yet, but I've found the old address and I hope to start looking today," came the reply.

"A lot depends on you. I've checked with our lawyer and he assures me that the fifty-year condition runs out in twenty three days."

"Don't worry Alex, I'll make sure no heir is found. Besides I'm looking forward to my hefty bonus." The connection wasn't very good and the voices echoed. "I'll call you again soon."

"Very well." Alexander Cheyne hung up just as his father entered the room. Duncan Cheyne, balding, red faced and walking with a cane sat down in the chair nearest his son. Alexander had taken over the running of the estate two years ago and although it had relieved his father of many tedious tasks since his stroke, Duncan Cheyne had no idea that his only child was slowly milking the family bank account to pay for his drinking parties and voracious gambling habit.

No one would find out, if Alexander had his way because as of September 14th the estate would rightfully be his to do with as he pleased while his aging father carried on enjoying the illusion that he was Laird of the manor.

Alexander smiled, "Good afternoon Father, I trust you slept well?" He motioned a servant to attend to his father and help with the ottoman he used daily to rest his legs.

"Aye, quite well for a change." A large man, Duncan Cheyne leaned back in his chair then waved the servant away. "The tea the doctor recommended is a great help."

Alexander smiled at his father's pleasure then poured himself another drink. The stroke hadn't been as debilitating as the last one five months ago, and

Duncan Cheyne still found walking difficult, but Alex had noticed that his father's ability to focus and attend to conversations had diminished somewhat from this last episode.

*   *   *

"I'm in a total block, Simon." Kate Pennington switched the phone to her left hand then swept back the blinds of her front window so she could see out. "I know I still have six weeks but what good is time if I don't have an idea?" The sun was streaking into the front door window causing the beveled glass to reflect coloured stripes on her beige carpet. "Just a minute, Simon, there's someone at my door." The Canada Post driver left the package after ringing the door bell, then returned to his small delivery truck. "Okay, I'll call you in a week."

A package. Thoughts of its contents puzzled her. She wasn't expecting anything in the mail. The truck had left by the time she opened the front door, the package left sitting on her front step bench. It was small, about the size of two loaves of bread side by side, wrapped with brown paper and tied securely with butcher twine knotted every few inches to reinforce the paper seams. The stamps were British and it had the usual international stickers applied to the front surrounding the address.

Curiously Kate carried the package into her

house and set it down on a table near her reclining chair. She stared at the address then realized the delivery man had left it at the wrong house. She knew most of her neighbours but didn't recognize the name scrawled across the centre, Connor Cheyne c/o 85 Church Street, Port Dalhousie, Ontario, Canada. Kate didn't recollect ever seeing a Church Street in the neighbourhood either. There was a Church Street down town but it wasn't in the smaller village of Port Dalhousie.

It only took a few minutes for her to find and call the local postal outlet at a nearby plaza. "Postal Department, how may I help you?" came a rehearsed voice after she had pressed the required extension.

"I just received a package that isn't mine," she explained. "It says, 85 Church Street, Port Dalhousie, I'm 85 Johnston Street."

"Just a moment and I'll check for you," came back a practised reply. She was gone a considerable time leaving Kate to listen to a muted instrumental, and then a voice of an older man came on the line.

"I hear you have a package for 85 Church Street, Port Dalhousie. This happens once in a while, but it's right."

"So it was delivered correctly?"

"Yes, Johnston Street used to be Church Street before the amalgamation." Kate listened as the senior postal worker explained that prior to 1961, the township of Grantham and the towns of Port Dalhousie, Merriton and St. Catharines had streets with similar names so once they joined into the city of St. Catharines some of the duplicates had to be renamed. “Obviously someone found an old address. I’m surprised it made it to its destination. Someone downtown must have been on the ball. Is there a return address?”

Kate turned the package checking for any other address that might be concealed by stickers or twine. “No, I’m afraid not.”

“Let me check the name for you,” he said. Kate spelled the last name so it could be checked, probably using the same 411.ca web site that people used on the Internet. “Well, there doesn’t seem to be any person by that name in Canada. What I would suggest, is that you bring it in to us and it will be sent to the undelivered package department in Toronto.”

“Thank you,” replied Kate. “You’ve been very helpful.” She clicked the off button on her phone then slumped down in her recliner staring at the package resting on the table in front of her.

Why was there no return address? Why was it addressed to ‘care of’? Did the sender not want it returned? She looked at the mass of stamps laid out in neat rows along the right hand corner of the package. The postal stamp was smudged but the word Edinburgh was printed in a circular design within the decorative stamp indicating date and time. The address script was shakily written.

Connor Cheyne. It was an unusual name. Someone had sent this, using the only address they had from the past, hoping it would find its way to Connor Cheyne. The 'care of' on the address implied an obligation on her part. Someone was entrusting the receiver with its delivery and now she found it difficult to think of it sitting in a dead-end room with other undeliverable packages. Kate suddenly felt a pang of responsibility for this forlorn package. It must have been important for someone to send it this far, someone who had known Connor Cheyne and wanted him to have it. She turned the package around again checking for any other writing. Maybe there was something inside that could help her find its owner. It probably wasn't something she should do as it wasn't addressed to her, and there was most certainly some law which would be broken, but that didn't deter her from thinking about how to open it.

She fingered the folded ends of the package secured by tape where the opening had been creased diagonally then folded downward before being attached along the bottom. Twine she had, so that was no problem. Wide clear tape she would have to buy, but if the inside offered a clue to the owner then maybe she would be forgiven this transgression. After cutting the twine it meant slicing the tape at the two ends. Leaving the horizontal seam in tact across the back it might be possible to slide the contents out through one of the ends. Twenty minutes later the package still lay on the table in front of her, only now one of the ends sealed with wide tape had been coaxed open. The tape had been peeled off the down turned folded paper and the twine which secured the package with its knots was spread out on the table.

Carefully Kate eased out the contents that were secured in the second covering of plastic. She paused. A funny feeling came over her as she looked at the plastic bag's contents but it was too late to regret her actions. She had opened the package.

The plastic was a light shade of blue. Its end was also folded over and secured by a large elastic band that encased the whole bundle. Without opening it further Kate could tell that the majority of its contents consisted of paper; envelopes stacked in neat bundles and photos that even through the blue plastic looked old and worn. She started to doubt the validity of opening the package and suddenly felt as if she was intruding but curiosity about the owner urged her on. The elastic snapped and disintegrated into several smaller pieces around her hand as she gently stretched it. It was obviously quite old and by the indentation on the plastic bag, had been placed there a while ago. The contents freed now, Kate reached inside the bag to pull the smaller packets out.

She hesitated. It wasn't too late to put everything back as it was, yet thinking of the package sitting unclaimed in a postal station's dead-end room, spurred her on. She convinced herself that maybe she would find something to help find the owner or perhaps the sender. With that noble intention she reached back inside the light blue bag.

# Chapter 2

A stack of letters bound with twine, a smaller stack of sepia toned photos, a small velvet blue pouch with a red drawstring, and a gold coloured box were now laid out on the coffee table next to the blue bag. She sat looking at the items in front of her, almost afraid to continue.

The address on the top letter bore the same address as the package, her address, only the lettering was firm with deliberate strokes. Something about the stamps caught her eye. There was a smudged postmark bearing the word Edinburgh as was on the parcel but she noticed the monarch's picture on the stamps was that of George VI. Her first clue now told her that the top letter was probably written before the coronation of the present Queen in 1953, and by its unopened appearance, she supposed it had not been delivered to the right person, though how this letter with its canceled stamps ended up in the package, was intriguing. She raised up the package's brown paper covering and checked the stamps-Queen Elizabeth, then she noticed that some were modern pictures of the Queen and some seemed much older as if they had been applied many years ago when the queen was much younger. Then she searched for the customs label below the address and checked it for the contents description. One word written in by a different hand spelled the word-Letters.

Kate picked up the bundle of letters and fanned the ends to check some of the postage. All were 1953 or older. Kate had supposed that Connor Cheyne must have lived in her house at one time but now she had an estimated time frame, 1939-1953, or possibly earlier. That is if the sender had the correct address to begin with. Lost in thought the ring of the phone startled her.

"Hi, Kel. No I haven't forgotten." Though in reality Kate had forgotten the blind date set up for her by her sister. It wasn't that Kate didn't want to meet someone new, as her sister often accused, but her focus had been on her mystery package and it had possessed her thoughts for almost four hours. "I'm just running a bit late, but I'll be ready by seven." According to Kelly Gordon this new man, like all the others Kate had met was the perfect match for her. He was single, tall with dark hair and mustache, thirty years old and had just published his second book, which according to Kelly made him the perfect match for her sister, at least this time they had something in common.

"Just one problem," said Kate, "my car's been acting up. Can you pick me up?" Intent that her plans not be upset again, her sister agreed to pick her up and take her to the restaurant herself. "Okay," said Kate, "see you later."

Kate glanced at the wall clock above the television. She had two hours left to get ready for another evening of boredom. Oh well, it came with a free meal so she could put up with expectant looks from Ted and Kelly and listen to "what's his name" while they pretended to be enjoying each others company. During the last few years Kate had lost herself in work and for a while work had helped lessen the pain but maybe now it was time to go forward, all she could hope for was that her sister's taste in men for her was improving.

Kate was already getting hungry having missed lunch but decided to get ready before rifling through the fridge for a snack to hold her over. Her bedroom clock chimed six-thirty while she was just fastening her outfit. Kate looked at herself in the bedroom mirror then glanced at the framed photo on her dresser. Evan. In two more months it would be three years.

His hair was a tousled light brown and his tan brought out the vivid blue of his eyes. "You know we said we would wait", he had said to her the day before. He'd taken her in his arms and tilted her chin up giving her a lingering kiss. "It won't be long now and I want our wedding night to be special, besides, Mum doesn't mind having her only son back home for a few months," he smiled at that thought. "It gives her someone to fuss over, with Dad gone."

Kate knew the moment she had first spotted him at a company party, that Evan was the one, and after four months together had reluctantly agreed to wait these next few months, to remain apart until their wedding. Their wedding.

She was a year older now than he was when he died. She thought back to their last goodbye, their last moment together. It had been a hurried hug and kiss at the door as the airport taxi waited. Evan had loved to ski. She remembered the phone call as vivid now as it had been then and how his mother had sounded when she told Kate of her son's death. Kate hadn't believed that Evan was gone. His body hadn't been found. Twice during the next week she was sure she had seen him at a local mall and each time she had hurried to catch up to the familiar blonde only to find she was mistaken. Then on March 20th Evan's mother had called. They had found Evan, his body partially hidden in a narrow crevice. The truth had hit her then. At that time she wished she had gone with him to the Rockies and had died with him in the mountains but now after three years the pain had lessened and her dashed hopes of marriage and happiness with the man she had loved seemed like a dream. Now, there were fewer days she cried for the loss and felt guilty because she had remained home and ...lived.

She blinked back a tear from her eye, then smiled fondly at the grinning face looking up at her from its frame. "Not bad for twenty nine." She left her dark hair down to hang loose about her shoulders. The black jump suit wasn't new although this was the first time she had decided to wearit. She liked the palazzo style of the legs and the jeweled, teal-green bolero jacket that matched her eyes. The door bell rang. Kelly must be really eager about this one. "Just a minute," she called. She smiled at her sister's enthusiasm.

After turning the lock she opened the oak door to find a stranger smiling at her with a small corsage in his hand. The smile broadened as Kate stood there just staring.

"There's been a change of plans, I'm afraid," he said meekly, not sure of his greeting.
"Ted had some difficulty at work and wasn't home yet, so Kelly called and asked that I come over and collect you myself."

Kelly hadn't said he was British but the rest of

her description didn't do him justice. Kate managed a sheepish smile. She was embarrassed now for the look of what must have been confusion and awe on her face as she opened the door. "Come in, please." He stepped inside then presented her with flowers, three small fabricated blooms formed from pale yellow gladiola petals on a bed of green.

"They're beautiful. Thank you." Kate slipped her left wrist through the elastic on the underside.

His eyes hadn't left hers. He held out his hand. "My name is Nightingale, Robin Nightingale." He smiled again, waiting for her reaction as her eyes widened at such a joke played on a young child. "My parents had an unusual sense of humour," he said. "My friends call me Birdie."

Kate laughed, "I like that. I'm Katherine Pennington but you can call me Kate." He nodded dutifully. "We have a little time, would you like a drink before we go?"

"Thank you, yes." From the kitchen Kate noticed as he glanced around the adjoining living room.

"I have some chilled white wine," she offered.

"That would be fine." He gravitated toward the tall book shelf at the far end of the living room and Kate could see him from the kitchen as he fingered some of her novels then turned toward her smiling. "Your sister said you were a writer but I had no idea," he waved his arm across the collection of her children's novels that took up two shelves, "that you were so accomplished."

"I've been very lucky," she said, passing Birdie his glass of wine. He politely sat on the chair adjacent to her. "It's fun writing for children."

Birdie took a sip of wine and seemed surprised by its flavour. "This is quite nice. Is it local?"

"Yes, we have several local wineries, many in Niagara-On-The-Lake and Vineland, but during the last few years new ones have opened up throughout Niagara." She made some room on the coffee table for their glasses by moving the package and its wrapping to the far end. "What brings you to St. Catharines?" she asked, curious as to how he came to meet Ted and Kelly but not wanting to ask directly.

"Actually I was to meet a friend and stay for a few weeks but as it turned out Geoffrey acquired a freelance assignment from Ted's firm and left for Vancouver last night." He took another sip of wine. "That's how I met Ted. Geoffrey is a photographer and did the photo work on my books, so when he went to the meeting at the Holiday Inn I tagged along intending to wait at the bar until he was finished."

"But as fate would have it," she summarized,

"you are now on your way to a restaurant with a woman you don't know in a city you don't know to meet a couple you just met last night."

"Well, in a nut shell, yes," he chuckled, "but as Geoffrey said I might use his flat, it seems I'll stay for a while at least." He looked at the remaining wine in his glass. "Maybe I could check out the local wineries, you know, give the tourist take on things here."

Kate liked listening to Birdie speak. She had always had a thing about accents and prided herself on being able to pinpoint a dialect, but his was different somehow. She caught herself staring at him and hoped he hadn't noticed as he seemed to be interested in the package now that was laid out at the end of the table. The stamped envelope pile sat still tied in a bundle next to the other unopened packages.

"Those look interesting."

Embarrassed to tell him the whole story and confess her crime, Kate simply nodded before having another sip from her glass.

"Well, shall we be going?" he asked, checking the time on his watch.

It was a beautiful August evening. Not too warm and only a slight breeze that felt refreshing on her face after her half glass of wine. She hadn't had a chance to snack earlier and was aware of the flushing effect. Birdie was the perfect gentleman and Kate couldn't remember the last time a man had opened a car door for her. Kelly's last arranged date had remained in his car and just honked the horn for her. Birdie's car was a rental yet roomy and luxurious. She noticed the gold ring on his right hand as he opened the door. "That's an unusual ring," she commented.

He hesitated before answering, "Yes, I found it in a pawn shop and thought it rather interesting," then he added, "I didn't pay much for it."

Conversation in the car driving over was light and Kate had discovered her escort lived in London but had spent many years in Edinburgh. She smiled thinking of the dialect she couldn't place. He had indeed published two books in as many years, both on touring in Ireland. They pulled into the restaurant a few minutes past seven but still managed to arrive before her sister and her husband.

Kate decided not to discuss the package during the dinner conversation. For now she would keep the owners search to herself. She was curious about Birdie though, and she questioned her sister about their meeting when the two adjourned to the ladies room after ordering. "Geoffrey spoke highly of him," assured Kelly, as if Geoffrey's recommendation was the only verification she needed that this stranger was an appropriate match for Kate.

"He does seem nice enough," agreed Kate, "maybe too nice." Her sister gave her one of those looks in the mirror while fixing her hair. Kelly had heard it all before, but also realized that all the criticisms and protests were Kate's way of protecting herself against the deep betrayal she felt even considering dating again. Hopefully she would find another love to take the place of the one she'd lost and Kelly didn't feel at all guilty in trying to push the time line along.

Kelly entwined her arm in Kate's and gave her a small hug. "It's just a supper date; you don't have to marry him. Just try to relax and have some fun. You haven't been out for over two months.

"Maybe you're right, besides he does seem pleasant enough." She returned the hug, "and you did choose a beautiful restaurant."

"C'mon, we have two handsome gentlemen waiting for us so let's just enjoy the evening."

Dinner took over two hours and the evening seemed to be going well. Kelly and Ted exchanged conspiratorial glances whenever the couple engaged in a common interest. Afterwards Birdie offered to drive Kate back to her home, which to the delight of Kelly and Ted, Kate accepted. The evening was still early yet Birdie declined an invitation to come in for a coffee, sighting the time change as an excuse and politely kissed Kate on the hand before leaving her front door.

"Did you invite him in?" was the first question from her sister on the phone an hour later.

"Not that it's any of your business, but yes." Kate paused to let her sister complete her interrogation, "and he said he was still feeling a little off from the flight and asked if he might call me another time." Kate paused again waiting for another question. "I said that would be nice and that's the end of it," Kate heard a beep from her portable phone indicating low battery and hurried her conclusion, "and I probably won't hear from him again."

She picked up the table phone and heard the bewilderment in her sister's voice. "No, I didn't say anything to him to turn him off. We just didn't click." Which wasn't entirely true, for Kate had found Birdie very attractive and had found it difficult to keep her eyes off him throughout their supper. She enjoyed his wit and sense of humour as well as his refined demeanor and hoped he would get in touch with her again, although she wasn't about to confess that to her sister. Instead she said, "Thank you both for a lovely evening. The restaurant was wonderful and I enjoyed the company, and that's more than you can say about the last blind date you arranged for me." Kate switched the phone to her left hand cutting off Kelly's response, and she sat on the couch looking at the package, then pulled her obsession closer. "Yes, he was quite charming and thank you for arranging the date. You never know, maybe we will get together again. Okay, talk to you later."

It was getting late so Kate didn't mind tying up the phone line while using her Internet. She was still on dial up and as she didn't use the computer much other than research, emails and banking, she hadn't seen the need to update yet. Her computer sat on a small desk in the corner of her living room next to the couch she was sitting on. After getting herself a glass of white wine Kate sat at the keyboard waiting as the Internet connection came into view. First she would check the same site the post office had checked and waited again as the results for Connor Cheyne came up on the site.

There were several Cheynes in Canada but none with the same first name. There were only two in Ontario and none of them were in her immediate area. One in Toronto, an Andrew and one Jonathan Cheyne in Ottawa. She made a note of the addresses and phone numbers listed then turned off the computer. She swiveled her chair around and faced the waiting package.

Connor Cheyne must have lived in her house

at some point and probably before 1953, but how could she find out? She thought about the different records that the government kept on the population. Census records would be ideal but records for 1951 wouldn't be available until 2051 so that wouldn't help. Maybe an elderly neighbour might remember a couple by that name and she thought of Les Whitmore who lived across the street. He was the only elderly neighbour on the street who had lived there before Kate moved in. Kate had spoken to him on several occasions regarding local history, so he would be her first attempt to find out more tomorrow.

Pleased with her first plan of attack she decided it had been a long day. It was late and it was time for bed. The phone rang, startling her. "Hello?" She wondered if it was her sister calling back. "Oh," she paused, "hello." Kate suddenly felt flustered, it was Birdie, "No, I was just getting ready." He had phoned to thank her for an enjoyable evening.

"I enjoyed this evening too," she said. She listened as he proposed a late morning brunch. "Yes, I'd like that. Tomorrow at ten then, goodbye." Kate suddenly felt excited. Birdie had called to make another date and she was suddenly aware of how much she wanted to see him again. Tomorrow would be an interesting day.

# Chapter 3

It was seven-thirty when Kate woke to the screeching sound of the garbage collection truck. She was tired and felt she could have slept for a few more hours. Thinking about the previous days events had prevented her from falling to sleep and it was almost two before she had drifted off. Quickly putting on her robe and slippers Kate hurried out the side door to put out her bag of garbage for the week and her green organic bin. Plastic, cans and cardboard she had placed on the curb last night as they were in no danger of being strewn about by raccoons looking for food bits.

Birdie was picking her up at ten so that left a few hours to get ready and question Mr. Whitmore about his former neighbours.

Widowed seven years ago, Les Whitmore was still active in the community. For eighty-nine he was considered in good health. He enjoyed his garden and had recently showed it on a guided garden tour. He was in his garden when she arrived at his back-yard gate, surrounded by flower beds featuring different varieties of flowers. Tall and thin he reminded Kate of a movie actor. His vision was impaired slightly but he smiled broadly as she approached the dahlia bed he was working in "Good morning, my dear."

"Good morning, Mr. Whitmore," she replied stifling a yawn. It was a cool morning but the sun was warmly shining, the ground was a little damp from the morning dew and Les Whitmore knelt on a foam pad that both helped him to keep dry and protect his knees from the grassy humps and hollows of the ground. Arthritis had plagued him for many years and working in his garden helped alleviate the stiffness. He was dressed in his usual gardening attire and armed with a small spade and a bucket for tossing in weeds.

He leaned on the metal hand rails that encased the foam kneeler and slowly got to his feet. "You're up early this morning, so this must be an important visit." Living across from the young writer Les Whitmore probably knew Kate's habits better than anyone else and she smiled at the deduction.

"Well, as a matter of fact it is rather an important visit." She picked up the bucket and spade and walked with the old man to a nearby seat that surrounded the one and only tree in the back yard. "I know you have lived here a long time," she began, "and I was wondering if you remember who might have lived in my house after the war?"

He looked thoughtfully at Kate, taking her question seriously. "Let me see," he paused for a moment as he sat down. "When I came back from the war in '45 there was on old couple living there. They were friends of my grandparents, Duff, was their name. After that it was bought by a man who lived there for a year or two. I was traveling at that time and wasn't home much, so I don't remember his name but when I came home later to stay, there was a young couple living there. I remember that because they had a child, a boy and my mother went over often to help the young wife with the little one."

Hoping not to stop the flow of memories, she asked, "Do you remember the year the young couple lived there?"

"Oh, must have been '49 or '50. They weren't there long." He took a handkerchief from his pocket and wiped his forehead. "Then Mr. Anderson and his wife bought it. They went to a nursing home a few years ago and their son rented the house, which leads us to you my dear." He smiled, pleased with his memory skills. "Might I ask why so much interest in your house and its former owners?"

Kate explained how the package arrived with a name of a person who no longer exists. She confessed her decision to open the package in hopes of finding the owner and her reason for asking his help.

"Well, it seems that you have two possible people; the young man with the wife and child or the man who bought the house after the Duffs." He looked intrigued by the mystery. "Any ideas as how to find out?"

"You were my first choice,"

He nodded in agreement, "I think I'm probably the only one on the street who can go back that far." He thought for a moment before continuing, "Have you called city hall yet?" They had moved now back over to the dahlia bed and Les prepared to return to his weeding. "Maybe the tax department could be of some help."

"I'll try that next, but you've been very helpful." Kate waited until he was comfortably positioned on his foam kneeler before handing him the bucket and spade.

"Thank you," he said. "Do let me know how it turns out."

Kate was motivated now, "I will, and thank you for your help."

There was still time before she was to leave so she hurriedly looked up the city hall number. It seemed a long time before it was answered by a pleasant sounding woman who asked how she could be of help. Kate explained that she would like to find out who lived in her house before she had moved in and after a slight pause the woman replied, “I think the assessment roll would be your first place to try. I’ll give you the number.”

Twenty minutes later Kate was at the garden gate, smiling excitedly. Mr. Whitmore was still in the dahlia garden and had made some progress in eliminating the weeds in his bed. From a distance the red blooms resembled a thicket of deep red roses among the dark green foliage. He smiled at her excitement. “Well, you look like you had some luck.”

“Quite interesting really; I learned that if you call city hall enough times you finally find what you’re looking for.”

“So you found the names you were searching for?”

“Not exactly, but I did find out where to look.” Kate spread her jacket on the grass next to her elderly neighbour then sat down. “I called city hall first and they directed me to the tax assessment department, who, because they only have the current rolls told me to call city hall back and ask for the tax department.” Kate repositioned her legs on her coat sleeves. “The lady at the tax department was very interested and quite eager to help me, especially when I explained I was researching a book.” She gave Mr. Whitmore an impish look. “Apparently the old tax assessment rolls are kept up at the university. And, here’s the neat part, she said the older records probably would have renters names included as well as the owners.”

“Well I guess you will be making a trip to Brock sometime soon then.”

Kate smiled. She had called Brock University and received the same courteous helpfulness. “Yes, I spoke to the library archivist and she said to come anytime.”

Mr. Whitmore looked up, “It looks like you have some company.” It was ten o’clock and Birdie had pulled up into Kate’s driveway.

“Oh! Brunch date,” she smiled, “I better go.” She brushed off her pants and shook out her jacket. “Thanks again for your help.”

As Birdie was new to the area it was decided that Kate would choose the brunch location. There was a small cafe not far from her house on the outskirts of the village and after a brief drive they settled into a cozy booth furthest from the door.

Kate decided on broccoli quiche, something she hadn’t had for a long time, while Birdie chose sausage and eggs with Canadian bacon.

“What are your plans now that you’ve been abandoned in the city?” she asked smiling.

“None really, except perhaps to check out the

wineries."

Relaxed compared to last evenings supper Kate noticed he seemed younger than she had thought. He dressed well, but in jeans, a sweater and a jacket, he appeared more at ease. He caught her looking at him and smiled. "Why, do you have something in mind?" Half way through his eggs he had noticed a cruet of Canadian maple syrup sitting on the table and decided he had to try it by ordering a side order of pancakes. Kate smiled at his appetite and laughed at his exaggerated enjoyment of the pure maple syrup.

"Maybe." She wondered what Birdie would think of her amateur sleuthing and decided she would confide in him. "Yesterday I found a package, or rather the package found me. It belongs to someone who no longer lives in my house."

"Is that the package I saw on your table last night?" he asked, before loading up the last bit of bacon on his fork.

"Yes. I had planned to open up one or two of the letters to see if they would give me a clue to the person's whereabouts." After the last of the quiche Kate explained how she had found out the previous owners from Mr. Whitmore and her success with the tax department.

"What if the old address is wrong and the

package was actually meant to be delivered somewhere else?"

Kate had thought about this possibility before. "That's one of the reasons I want to check the tax records. I guess I'm curious and if his name is listed there then maybe there might be another person's name listed as well that might help."

Birdie seemed intrigued, he'd stopped eating to listen to her story and his brown eyes were intent on hers, "I've done a little genealogy research on my father's family, maybe I could be of some assistance."

"I'd like that."

"So are we off to the university then?"

"Right after you finish that last pancake." Kate was excited. She had found a co-conspirator and she welcomed the company.

It didn't take long to find a parking space. Classes were breaking for lunch and Kate was able to spot a place in a lot not too far from the library tower.

During their fifteen minute drive Kate had revealed more about the mysterious package and her thoughts about the postage and contents. "I'm not sure if we will find anything useful in the records," she confessed, "Connor must be pretty old by now if he's still alive."

"If we find him, at least you will have some confirmation that he did live in your house. If

nothing else you can always re-wrap the package and send it to the post office."
Kate nodded in agreement.

They were quiet for a moment as Birdie pulled into a vacant parking spot. "So do you think your Connor Cheyne is Scottish or Canadian?" Kate hadn't thought about that and had just assumed he was Scottish, but either seemed a possibility.

Once parked, Birdie opened the door for her and together they walked the short distance to the library entrance. Crossing the road that separated the parking area from the main grounds Birdie instinctively took Kate's hand as a passing car came a little too close to their side of the road. Kate shifted her bag, the one she usually carried when she was doing research that contained her purse and a few writing utensils along with writing pads. She gave the car's driver a dirty look even though it was long past then grinned at Birdie. "I've only had the package a short time and already I'm a target.

He smiled, then joining in he replied, "I've only been here a day so I doubt they know about me yet. It has to be you they're after." Then they both laughed.

A young librarian greeted them and Kate asked for the archivist Gayle Morton. After a few minutes they were led to the second floor where the records Kate wanted were housed. Gale Morton showed them the microfilm machine they would be using and explained how to find the film they were seeking. The records for those years were divided by town, year and then streets.

Patiently Birdie scrolled down the numerous house descriptions until he came to Kate's street. Kate sat in a chair next to him and gazed intently at the names listed under each property.

"There," she said, "Church Street." But the number of houses on the street didn't correspond to the current houses. Some hadn't been built until the fifties.

"Go back again," she suggested, "and then we can look for the Duff couple."

"This looks like it," said Birdie as he slowly brought the page into focus. The house listed Andrew and Abby Duff as owners in 1945 and the house description matched Kate's current home. It took less than five minutes to find the next assessment that showed the Duffs again as the owners. Kate passed Birdie the next reel and as they searched through the years they again found her house description listing a William Cousins as the owner and as she had hoped, it showed the name of the tenant, Mrs. Ann Springate. Kate noted that the ownership listed only William Cousins and made no reference to a wife as co-owner as with the Duffs, so maybe he was not married.

They scrolled to the next assessment year and Kate gasped softly as she saw her house listed in 1950. She read the information as Birdie enlarged the owner/occupier area. William Cousins was still the owner but with new tenants, 'Mr. and Mrs. C. Lyonne.'

"Is that the name you were looking for?" asked Birdie.

Disappointed now, Kate slumped back into her chair. "No, I was hoping for Connor Cheyne."

"Let's make sure," said Birdie and he scrolled on to the next assessment year to confirm what Mr. Whitmore had told her. The house had sold again and the names of George and Alice Anderson were now the sole owners and occupants of the house.

"Well I guess the address on the package must be wrong and if it is then we will never know if there is someone at another address who would know about the Cheynes." she concluded a little saddened, now that her search had not helped locate the owner of the package.

"I don't know," said Birdie. With a hint of a smile he leaned back in his chair so he could face Kate. "With my Father's family, I had a great, great, great grandfather who went by his middle name of Ian which really threw me off the trail for a while. Then I got a copy of his death certificate giving his parents names and date of birth which corresponded with the information I had for a William." Kate looked puzzled. "What had happened was, that he had had an older brother named William who died, then his parents had him six years later and named him William. I guess when he grew up he didn't want to have his dead brother's name so he went by Ian instead. Funny thing was that none of his sons had the name Ian, but the eldest one was a William."

Kate still didn't quite understand how this story applied to her search. "What are you suggesting?" she said finally.

Birdie broadened his smile, "Nothing really. I just like telling that story."

Kate just shook her head and smiled then sat in the empty chair next to Birdie. "How to find someone that the post office says doesn't exist, or their family?" She was silent for a moment while Birdie slowly rewound the film back on its reel. "Maybe if we had marriage information for Connor Cheyne or a death record with an address," then a little enthusiastically, "or maybe he was Scottish as you suggested and went back home."

Birdie wrapped the end securely around the reel as he edged it off the machine. "At home most of the British census records and the births, deaths and marriages are on the Internet now, but I'm not sure if it's true for the Canadian records." He replaced the film in its box and handed the boxes they had searched back to Kate. "You could try the Mormon Church if there is one locally or perhaps their LDS web site."

Kate carried the stack of microfilm boxes back to the main desk where Gayle Morton sat searching on her computer and thanked her very much for her help and then she asked, "If I was looking for a Canadian marriage or a death, how would I go about it?"

Gayle Morton thought for a moment then suggested, "The main library downtown has the Ontario information. I would try there first."

Excited now that she had a new direction to follow, Kate and Birdie left the University library. Fat fluffy clouds floated their way toward the east as the sun made an effort to shine between them creating a succession of light then shadow.

"Maybe I was right all along. Maybe I should focus on the contents of the package first or at least call the Cheyne names I found in the phone book." She gave Birdie a look of uncertainty.

"I'm at your service, Milady." He said, giving a hint of a bow. We can go to the library now or go back to your place and call the library from there or do as you suggested and look at the letters for some clue first. Then again we could go for a bite to eat." With this, he gave her a sheepish look.

"What about a snack and some coffee? I know a nice place in Port Dalhousie," she said smiling.

Birdie looked at her thoughtfully for a moment, "Make it tea instead and I'm yours."

# Chapter 4

Kate sat the tray with tea pot, and accessories down on her coffee table and poured Birdie a cup of tea. She'd used her mother's china set and Birdie seemed impressed with her tea making skills. "My mother's English," she offered, reading his thoughts.

"Well, I like you better already," he smiled taking the proffered cup, "Where is she from?"

"Croydon, south of London. She met my father while he was visiting friends. They got married there then she came back with him in '81."

Kate had sliced some cranberry pound cake and together they enjoyed their snack. There were a few times when neither spoke but, unlike other dates she had had, Kate didn't feel awkward. She enjoyed Birdie's company. He made her feel relaxed without the need to be 'on' all the time.

The last crumb erased from his plate, Birdie sat back on the couch and looked curiously at the package. "Well, what is our next plan of attack?"

"I can phone the library now and see if we can look up a death or marriage certificate." Kate suggested.

Birdie helped himself to another cup of tea while Kate hunted for the Public Library phone number.

The phone rang but she felt she had pressed the wrong extension number. Birdie sat patiently and waited. "Hello, do you have a genealogy section in the library? Yes, thank you." Kate waited and glanced at Birdie who now had taken off his jacket and like Kate seemed eager to hear the results of her inquiry. "Hello, can you tell me if it is possible to see a 1945 marriage in Ontario?" She chose 1945 because that seemed a good point to start from. "Oh," she paused, "no, I'm not a relative. What about a death?" She waited while the librarian explained. "Okay, thank you."

She had scribbled some notes as she spoke to the librarian and after hanging up she gave Birdie the bad news. "It looks like we're out of luck."

Birdie nodded anticipating the information that was given, "I know, privacy issues." He sat down with his cup of tea, "It's the same in Scotland."

"It's interesting though," she said a little disappointed. "I did learn something, births go up to 1909, marriages to 1924 and deaths to 1934."

"So if our couple were married in 1924 we would be able to find them. Too bad they weren't English, their records go up to 1983." Like Kate he was now staring at the package sitting before them at the end of the table.

She reached out and picked up the small gold coloured jewellery box and sat it gently on the table between the two of them then raised the lid slowly. Smaller fabric bags filled the space and Kate picked one up and loosened the tiny drawstring that held the contents inside. She reached in and pulled out a heavy metal star and placed it right side up with its attached ribbon laying flat about it. "Medals," she said in wonderment. "I wonder if they belonged to Connor.

"Most likely," answered Birdie. "These are British," he continued as Kate laid out the four shapes. "I know this one," he said," It's the 1939-45 Star"

Kate handled the brass coloured star carefully, "So that means he was in the war from 1939-1945."

"Not necessarily, it's for six months service any time between those years."

"So he could have joined in 1944 and still get this medal, which might make him younger than we think." She carefully placed the medals back into their protective bags.

"Well, we could also look for all the medals on line and see which campaigns they were for and get a more precise date." He placed the bags back into the jewellery box, “That would probably be very interesting but wouldn’t help with finding him here in Canada.”

Kate reached over and picked up the small stack of photos that rested in the bottom half of a small brown cardboard box. The top one was very old and the dress of the woman seated in an elegant chair with furs draped over her shoulders, and a wide fur trimmed hat suggested the early twentieth century or perhaps the eighteen nineties. The next was of an army officer. A young man standing in his best uniform, against a tall table. “I wonder if this is Connor?” she asked, passing the photo to Birdie.

Birdie looked at the photo thoughtfully, “It looks as if it could be. This is a World War II Army Lieutenant and he seems the right age,” concluded Birdie. “The woman might be his mother or Grandmother although there doesn’t seem to be much of a family resemblance.” He turned over the photos to see if anything had been written about the subject on the back but both were empty. The name of the Edinburgh photography studio was written across the bottom of the older picture, which in itself he found interesting.

Kate reached for the bundle of letters and fanned them slowly wondering which one to open first. She looked at the picture of the young soldier.

There were two letters with no address on them but each had the word Father written across the front and a military 'Passed by Censor' stamp below it. She slid these two out carefully intending to replace them if it helped in their search. Birdie had moved closer to her now and together they sat expectantly as Kate removed and unfolded the first letter. "Oh," she said, surprised at its condition. It was a short letter due to the fact that most of it was missing. A large section near the middle had been carefully snipped out and a few lines both above and below were missing. "This Censor seemed to enjoy his job." It was dated October 1939.

*Dear Father,*

*It has been two weeks since leaving our base. Our training here continues* –**this part was cut out-** *but everyone is optimistic. I am in the company of wonderful companions. All, including myself, await the moment we might fight this evil that threatens our homeland. Grandfather would be proud of us. I know Mother will continue to worry about me but all is well and I think of you both. Everyone here is of the opinion that* **-there was a large hole cut out of the central part of the letter, leaving only the remaining line-***hopefully I shall be home in time for Mother's birthday.*

*All my love,*

*Connor*

"It sounds as if he was part of the British Expeditionary Force sent to Belgium in '39," offered Birdie.

"So the cut out part of the letter was for security reasons then?" Birdie nodded. They were quite strict about what information you could send home in a letter.

"He and his friends seem so eager," she said sadly, "so proud to be there. If only they knew."

"I suppose young men, boys actually, have this romantic view of war, glory and all that." replied Birdie. "And it doesn't help that the recruitment methods make you feel somewhat a coward, or pro enemy, if you didn't join up with your friends."

Kate gave a saddened sigh at the hopeful anticipation of a young soldier. She glanced at Birdie who had the same look as each knew what had and possibly would happen to the many young men sent to war. He waited patiently for the realization to fade as she opened up the second letter. It was dated May 1, 1940 and as the previous letter, had been stamped with the Censor's stamp.

As with the first, this letter had also been sent within another letter or package. It was creased badly and worn as if it had been read many times over. There were maroon coloured smudges toward the top of the page and Kate realized they had originally been smudges of blood.

*Dear Father,*

*Tell Mother that I love her and that I am safe.* **As with the other letter there was a large strip of print cut out at this point. -***as a day I shall never forget...for all of us. Our first day of battle. Our forces were –* **here the print was blackened out-** *and for the first time we saw the enemy. I lost a dear friend and the thought of it fills me with sorrow. Edmond died in my arms after a short skirmish with a patrol of enemy soldiers. Two of my men were blown apart by grenades. Edmond was close by and remains of shrapnel tore into his neck. I found him lying in his own blood. Luckily his loss of blood was quick as it had torn through the artery and he had little pain. I wondered then if he realized he was dying. He was still conscious as I promised to write his mother and Allie. Then he looked at me as I held him suddenly knowing he would never see his wife again. I tried not to, but tears came and he smiled when they dropped to his cheek.*

*This is not what I thought it would be like, so close and personal. I saw the face of the man I killed today. He was young, as we all are. His terrified look, when he hesitated and saw my rifle raised, as if he knew he was dead already.*

*Tell Grandfather I understand now, all those times he didn't want to speak of the war he had been in when I had asked him so innocently as a child. My hands shake with the memory and I pray that I will be able to face what comes with the courage to lead my men.*

*Tomorrow-***There was another large space cut away then it resumed-***I pray I survive the days to come.*

*I enclose Edmond's few personal effects.*

*Your loving son,*

*Connor*

Kate set the letter down, both of them silent for a moment. Tears blurred her eyes but she blinked them back.

Birdie picked up the photo of the young soldier, "He must have been with the forces that retreated from the beaches at Dunkirk."

She looked at the picture Birdie held, "I wonder what Connor did before the war? It must have been so hard for them, so young and expected suddenly to kill other men" She carefully refolded the letter and set it on top of the first one they had read.

Kate picked up the third letter. It was still sealed, unopened, and yet had been apparently delivered as showed by the canceled stamps. The address was the same as the package address although this was addressed directly to Connor Cheyne.

The envelope was a pale blue, the old fashioned kind that folded up after writing in it then the sides were glued over closing the edges. On the back was a space for the return address which had been left blank. "I need a knife," Kate quickly went to the kitchen and came back with a small paring knife. She hesitated, glancing at Birdie who nodded slightly, then carefully slit the seam along the two sides. It was dated June 7th 1950.

*My Dearest Son,*

*It is with great sadness that I write to tell you that your father has died today. His doctor reports that his heart gave out while he was sleeping. It was a blessing for him. The last few years had been difficult for him as you know, the headaches had increased in severity and there were days that he himself wished death as the doctors could do nothing for him. We now know that a tumor had caused much of his pain, but at last now he is at peace. I hope you can find it in your heart to forgive him after all these years. I know now it was probably the disease that had affected his mind.*

*I fear now that your Grandfather will despair. He is unwell and fears for his home. I have convinced him now that you did not die in the war, even though I have no proof as your Father destroyed your letters as well as any Army correspondence. I am now unable to see your Grandfather as your Uncle is pressing upon him and wishes to assume power of attorney and as such, your inheritance. Please let us know you are alive and well before it is too late.*

*I pray for this with all my heart.*

*Your Loving Mother.*

Kate was silent, staring at the letter. She remembered vividly Evan's mother's voice, how she had sounded in the depth of sorrow and was suddenly aware of the anguish this mother must have felt and her eyes started to gloss over. "He never knew his father died," she said in a whisper, "He never opened the letter."

Birdie didn't say anything and just put his arm around her shoulder then after a few moments he gave her a little hug. "We don't know that for sure, yet it does seem that was the case." He took the letter from her hand and folding it again as it was, placed it next to the remaining stack of letters. Both were quiet, suddenly realizing now that they had entered into someone's life, and had felt the tragedy and despair that they had felt.

Kate was confused as this seemed to indicate that Connor Cheyne had indeed lived in this house if his mother had sent him letters. Maybe he just stayed with the owners or rented a room, or perhaps it too was meant to be delivered to a neighbouring house. She wished now they had checked the houses next to hers at the library while they were going through the reels of film.

"The letter was unopened so maybe it was the wrong address," she said aloud, then looked at Birdie, "But there's no return address so it couldn't have been sent back by the Post Office. So how did it get in the package?" Birdie gave a slight shrug.

Kate reached for the next letter in the pile. She looked at Birdie for approval, who nodded, "Might as well." he said.

Kate used the paring knife again and carefully unfolded the fourth letter dated May 21st 1950.

*My Dearest Son,*

*Spring has come to our home early this year. Frederick says we will soon have a new foal.*

Kate read as Connor's mother told of their hardships after the war, politics, gardens and every day life in post war Britain. Birdie followed along silent as Kate read, then came to the important part of the letter.

*Your Father still refuses to admit your existence to your Grandfather. He is a stubborn, bitter man and would rather see his father's estate go to his brother than give hope to your Grandfather that you are still alive. He continues to insist that you have died in the war and has intercepted any proof I might show your Grandfather. He is more explosive now and the fits of anger have become more violent. I sometimes think I should ask the doctor to intercede on my behalf but he has witnessed none of this behaviour and would probably be reluctant to take further steps other than the pain medication he prescribes for headaches.*

*Your sister is well and lives now with her in-laws. Your Father has driven her away from our home by his actions. He has forbidden me to speak of you and I am powerless to help. The war has left a mark on us but I fear it has crippled your Father's mind since you left. Please write as I long to hear from you.*

*As always,*

*Your Loving Mother*

Kate lowered the letter, "How sad," she said.

"Come on now." encouraged Birdie. "We opened these for a reason, so let's see what we've learned."

Kate smiled, "You're right." Once more focused she reached into her bag and pulled out a larger note pad. "Okay, so what have we got?"

Birdie thought for a moment, "Let's put it down like a family tree chart. We know there is a grandfather so put him at the top. Now draw a short line down from the grandfather then a horizontal line with two short vertical lines at the ends showing Connor's father and uncle." Birdie showed her where the 'names' of the two brothers, father and uncle, should be on the graph then put little equal signs next to their spots then two more short horizontal lines allowing a place for the wives later if found.

Under Connor's father they placed the date of death as November 1950. Next he drew a vertical line under this couple then another horizontal line with two short lines at the ends where he wrote Connor's name below one and the word sister below the other. Pleased with himself he sat back and admired his handiwork.

"There, Connor Cheyne's family." Kate nodded understanding now how the chart went. "Now it would seem that the Uncle is the baddie at this point and is trying to take Connor's inheritance. We know his sister was married so I will add a place in for her husband." Kate watched as he added an equal sign by the name sister then another vertical line with the word baby below it. "Now we're only assuming that the father died in Scotland because of the letter, so let's put 'Scotland ?' next to the date." Birdie finished the family chart by adding the words 'bad guy' in brackets next to the word uncle then handed the chart to Kate for inspection.

"How old do you think Connor was in 1950?" she asked.

"Well, he was in the war so if he was eighteen he could have been born around…" Birdie sketched a quick calculation on his palm, "1921, or earlier if he was older in 1939."

"So at twenty nine or thirty he would probably have a family."

They sat on the couch facing the package's various components. "I don't understand," said Kate. "If his mother had these medals, aren't they proof that he lived through the war. Why couldn't she just have shown these to the grandfather?"

"Don't forget, Connor's mother has probably been dead for many years, and we don't know who sent the package to this address so we don't know that she ever saw these. Then changing the subject he said, "What about a break? I hear you live in a beautiful city and I am in need of a tour guide. If you haven't other plans perhaps we can get together later."

Kate's face brightened. "I guess I do need a break. We've done a lot today." Kate noticed her clock. "Look! It's almost four o'clock"

Birdie was standing now and putting on his jacket. "It's been a fun afternoon. Thank you for including me in your hunt. I'm just sorry we didn't accomplish much." He held Kate's hands in his then leaned forward and kissed her on the cheek. "Shall I collect you at six then."

"I'd like that."

# Chapter 5

It was late. Alexander Cheyne was just putting down his book when the phone next to his bed rang. "I didn't expect to hear back from you so soon. This must mean you have some news."

"Just enough to know I made the right decision. I now know who has the package. I also checked the land registry office and there is nothing there to imply he even existed."

"Good, keep me informed." With that Alexander Cheyne smiled then hung up the phone.

* * *

Kate watched as Birdie got into his car then pulled out of her driveway. She watched as he drove down the road and wondered what sort of man he was. She liked him. They definitely had a mutual attraction and she was eager to spend more time with him. Kate had two hours before Birdie would return, more than enough time to get ready. She went back to her couch and sat in front of the package's contents. It was intoxicating, maybe she would open one more.

Then she looked at the small blue velvet

pouch. It had stiffened with age but she could feel there was something small inside. Slowly she pulled the thin red cord that held the pouch closed and tumbled out the contents onto the flattened brown wrapping of the package.

A gold ring with a crest. It was a man's ring. Kate fingered the object and studied the crest. It looked like some sort of cat standing on its hind legs with front feet pawing the air. Kate had seen this crest somewhere else before. She tried the ring on the middle finger of her right hand then it came to her… Birdie. A shiver ran down her body and suddenly she felt uneasy. She was sure he wore a ring like this, in fact she had even commented on the cat in the centre. This seemed more than a coincidence but then maybe she was making too much of it. There had to be many cat or lion designed rings on the market today. Maybe they were just similar.

There were words above the animal- Sans Peur. French words- Without Fear. Kate tried hard to remember if Birdie's ring had such writing, but couldn't. She wondered what he would say if he saw the ring then decided to put it back in the pouch without saying anything, then wait and see. She checked the clock, there was still lots of time.

Kate looked at the stack of letters. The next letter in the pile looked as the previous two did but this one had tears down the sides similar to the cuts she had made with the paring knife. This one had been opened and read, yet it was addressed to the same person. Looking further she noticed that the stamps had been cancelled which meant it had also been delivered but to a different address: Netley Hospital Hampshire. Carefully Kate pulled out the letter and opened the faded blue paper. It was dated May 4, 1944.

*My Dearest Connor,*

It was a lengthy letter telling of life missed on a vast estate. It told of friends, gardens, how the war had changed their country, and the rations that were now a part of everyday. Their large home had twice been used for billeting soldiers, and English ones at that, his mother had complained. Several of the homes in the town had London evacuees staying with them while life in London was still so uncertain. Kate read on quickly until she reached the real reason for the letter.

*We are told the war will soon be over and I pray you stay safe until then. I am ever thankful your wound is not serious and that you are recovering well. We received word yesterday that Thomas has died in Italy. Hannah is heart broken knowing that he will never have seen his baby girl. She has received a few of his personal effects and sleeps with them near her bedside.*

Kate felt her eyes begin to blur. What did she have of Evan? They had talked about children as all couples do, about to be married. Evan had wanted a little girl, had even thought of a name he liked, she smiled at the thought of a little girl named Gwendolyn. The smile faded and the hurt returned. She thought about a child they could never have together. Was it better this way; not having a child to remind her daily of her loss. She sighed, "Poor Hannah."

*Your father has forbidden us to speak of you and she has threatened to leave and go to her husband's people. I fear I have lost my children forever.*

*Your father is a fool but I can say nothing to make him change his mind. He is determined that you are to do as he asks and marry Alice. Your grandfather longs to see you and I would entreat you to come home and talk to your father before you return to your unit. Please rethink you marriage.*

*May God keep you safe,*

*Your loving mother.*

The phone rang. "Hi, no, I'm almost ready," Kate lied. "Casual should be fine, okay, twenty minutes, bye." Kate felt flustered. Birdie would be back in twenty minutes. Ordinarily she would have been flattered that such a handsome man was eager to see her so soon but now she had mixed feelings. She wasn't sure how she felt about anything right now. There were only a few minutes to get ready before Birdie arrived. Kate picked up the next two letters in the pile and together with the one she had just read, put them in her bag to look at later. Hurriedly she fixed her hair and face ready for her next outing and changed into a pair of black slacks with matching top trimmed in blue.

Then she had an idea. Quickly she turned on her computer. As soon as the desk top came up she clicked on her internet connection. "C'mon," she said, hoping the door bell wouldn't ring yet. Eventually the Google screen came up and she quickly typed in 'family crest sans peur'. A moment later the screen filled with various choices based upon her search.

She chose the Wikipedia site, a free encyclopedia site that she had used often and seemed to know everything there was to know about everything. The screen switched to a new page, then there it was, the same picture that was on the ring. Picking up the ring she compared the cat and motto. They were identical. It belonged to the Sutherland clan. Kate bookmarked the page just in case she was forced to close it before she was finished. It outlined the history of the clan from the twelfth to the eighteenth centuries. She felt her heartbeats quicken, then the door bell rang. Kate abruptly shut off her computer. Her mind was racing.

Birdie stood at her front door grinning. "What's so funny?" she asked, through the screen matching his expression.

"I was just thinking, this is the most time I have ever spent with anyone on a second date."

"Well, technically it's our third," corrected Kate, letting Birdie in after unlatching the screen. He was dressed in faded jeans and a black Rugby shirt. His dark hair was swept back and he did indeed look good. Kate had forgotten for a moment about the ring then glanced at his right hand, but Birdie was no longer wearing the gold ring she had seen earlier. "Did you loose your ring?" she asked hoping she had sounded casual.

Birdie looked at his empty hand, "Must have, or maybe it's somewhere in Geoffrey's flat," he answered without real concern. His nonchalant response cleared up any suspicions Kate had about the ring. Then as if he just remembered, "I thought we might have a picnic, so I took the liberty." He set down the basket he had been holding in his left hand.

"That sounds very nice," said Kate, pleased that Birdie had taken the initiative. "Why don't we start with the town. There are shops, a beach, the pier and of course our famous carousel." Kate's black outfit didn't quite fit for the beach. "Here, have a seat and I'll change into jeans." It took less than five minutes for Kate to change into her favourite jeans and green top. When she returned to the living room Birdie was sitting dutifully on the couch waiting.

He smiled when she came out of the bedroom. "Much better." He picked up their lunch and wine. "Shall we walk or drive?"

"Let's walk. It promises to be a beautiful evening and it's not far. I have a bottle of soda water in the fridge, I'll bring it along."

They spent some time in the small stores that edged the tourist area of the town. Birdie bought some pure maple syrup that he intended for his mother though how much of it she would eventually get to taste Kate wondered. He enjoyed the small harbour with its many sailing boats and marveled how many visitor boats were tied up to the pier, their occupants partying as if they were in their own back yard. After a leisurely stroll down the pier they found a grassy area near the beach that was sheltered by a stunted tree where Birdie opened up his basket.

The picnic kit included a thin checkered plastic-coated cloth that was meant to replicate the old-fashioned picnic blanket, two melamine plates, two plastic glasses and cutlery. Not part of the kit but nestled in the food storage area of the basket were two kinds of cheese, bread and a package of ham slices. Birdie spread out the meal on the plastic 'blanket' then offered to open the bottle of white wine. Kate added soda water to her glass making a light wine cooler. The sun was lower in the sky now. It had been a beautiful day and the cooler temperatures earlier had given way to a warmer evening.

The sun rested on the watery horizon. The lake waters were calm with only the hint of an occasional ripple. People strolled along the shore, many in bare feet enjoying the feel of the sand as they walked. Children in bathing suits searched for colourful stones along the waters edge. Some people played Frisbee in the more open area near where Birdie and Kate were sitting. The music of the carousel gave the park a carnival feeling and the two watched as young and old, many who remembered the rides from their childhood, waited their turn to sit on the antique animals, animals that have been going round and round for years making people happy.

The sun was sliding ever faster now behind the horizon and in doing so lit up the sky with a pink glow. Dusk had come to Lakeside Park and Kate could hear the music in the near by bars and restaurants start up as the night crowd slowly made their way in. A breeze stirred the waters edge and Kate felt a shiver. Birdie had packed up now and found space to place the bottles in the centre. They walked back to the main sidewalk area hand in hand, his hand strong and warm in hers.

Birdie set the basket down on one of the many wooden park benches that dotted the park area. “Thank you for a wonderful day,” he said softly, his brown eyes looking into hers. “It had everything; adventure, good food, mystery and beautiful scenery,” he paused, his hand brushed against her cheek, “well, almost everything.” His face softened, then taking Kate’s hand drew her toward him. Kate hesitated a moment then she leaned in to give him a hug. Birdie tilted her chin up and stared into her green eyes. He felt her hesitate and draw back a little. He wanted to kiss her, to feel the tenderness of her lips on his. Instead he raised her hand to his mouth, smiled and brushed his lips in a gentle kiss across her fingers.

A chill ran through her. Kate smiled warmly in return then took his hands in hers. “You’re right, it’s been a wonderful day.” She slowly moved his hands around her to a place at her back as she moved closer to him. He reacted by holding her tighter and drawing her near. She could smell the musk of his cologne and the softness of his moustache as she leaned in closer. It was a very long kiss, gentle yet firm. She felt herself melt into him as he held her. She suddenly felt, she didn't quite know what she felt, she had been so alone for so long.

Birdie had recovered from their embrace and smiled warmly at her. "What now?" he asked softly, "I saw a nice looking restaurant by the water, we could sit and talk some more."

"We could do that at 85 Johnston Street too, besides I know the owner.

Clutching the basket in his left hand, Birdie held out his free arm to her, "Very well, Milady." They were quiet as they walked the few minutes back to Kate's place, her arm entwined in his. It was almost dark now and Kate felt happy. She had forgotten all about the letters she had carried around with her and now realizing they hadn't mentioned the package during their date, decided there would be time for that when they got back to her place.

The key wouldn't fit the lock on her front door and when Kate tried again forcing it more, the door let go of its grip and swung open without the benefit of key. "Did you leave your door unlocked?" asked Birdie in a low voice.

"No." she answered quietly, suddenly grasping his intent. She was confused, a dozen things going through her mind. Birdie held Kate back now and entered the house before her. There was no sound to indicate there was anyone in the house but that didn't mean someone wasn't waiting quietly in one of the other rooms. Purposefully Birdie dropped the shopping catalogue that sat on the deacons bench in the small foyer hoping to alert anyone that might be there that the owner had arrived home, then stepped backwards outside onto the front steps.

Kate was already down the steps waiting by Birdie's car. She was nervous but was alert enough to start dialing the local police department.

Birdie joined her, "Wait," he said. "Let's be sure first." There was no point in alerting the police if it was only a faulty door lock. They waited…there was no noise. "I'll go around to the back and see if anything looks disturbed," offered Birdie. Kate nodded in agreement and stood by the car while Birdie went up the sidewalk leading to the back yard.

Mr. Whitmore from across the street was standing in his screened porch. He had seen the two arrive and was curious now as to why Kate was standing outside by the two cars and why her friend had left her to go around the back. "Is there anything wrong?" he inquired after his wave got Kate's attention.

She was breathing hard with the excitement and took a moment before explaining, "We think someone has broken into my house." She glanced back to see if Birdie had returned. "Have you noticed anyone around during the last few hours?"

"Around six-thirty, I came out to put water in the birdbath." He stood next to Kate now both watching her house for signs of movement. "A car pulled in your drive. A man got out and went up to your door and a moment after, the door opened and he went in." Mr. Whitmore sat down on the top step now. "I thought you were home, the two cars were there so I didn't think much of it." Kate could see he felt badly. "I could have called the police if I had known."

"Did you see him leave?" asked Kate, now hoping she had proof that the house was free of burglars.

"Actually he wasn't there longer than two or three minutes, then he left with a package under his arm. Again I thought you were home. I'm so sorry," he said. Kate put a sympathetic hand on his arm. "It would have been dangerous if you were home. I'm so glad you weren't hurt." Then as an after thought he asked, "Did he steal much?"

Kate saw Birdie now coming back to the front yard and waved him over. Birdie joined the two on the long front steps of Mr. Whitmore's porch and after brief introductions, Birdie proclaimed the premises to be safe to enter. Kate confirmed that after relaying Mr. Whitmore's observations.

"Thank you, Mr. Whitmore, I better go now and check my house." She saw the concern on his face. "Don't worry, I've got Birdie here to protect me." She glanced at Birdie who gave her a sheepish smile. Kate gave him a warm hug as a farewell and went back across the street with Birdie. The door was still open and the two entered cautiously. There was no sound. Immediately Kate saw the empty coffee table, "Look!" The package and all its contents were gone.

# Chapter 6

But Birdie was searching the house, checking the windows and any hiding places within each room. Kate was sitting on the couch staring at the table when Birdie came back into the room. He'd noticed the missing package. "Is there anything else missing?"

"I haven't looked yet," she confessed, staring at the empty table, "but I will now."

Kate glanced around the room. Her computer was where it always was and her stereo and television were still in their cabinets. "Don't thieves usually take the electronics in a house?"

"They usually go for that stuff first," confirmed Birdie, "maybe you better check your jewellery and anything else of value." Birdie searched the basement while Kate checked her bedroom then the bathroom cabinet where she kept her most used jewellery items.

Amazed and puzzled Kate rejoined Birdie in the living room. "Nothing else is missing."

Birdie was sitting now on the couch and glanced around the room. "There's more to this," he said in a tone that brought a shudder through Kate's body. "It appears that someone came in here specifically for that package."

"But why? You mean someone else wants to find out about Connor Cheyne?"

"It would seem so, although how he knew it was here is puzzling. It's too bad he got everything." said Birdie, a little saddened now that their time hunting was cut short as well as a little upset that they hadn't seen everything there was to see in the package before they went out.

The burglary forgotten for the moment, Kate retrieved her bag from the front entrance, then smiled secretly, "Not quite everything." She quickly sat down beside Birdie and presented the three letters she had had all along. "I meant to bring them out to show you but we were having such a nice time I forgot all about them." Kate handed him the letter she had already read and waited for Birdie to finish reading. He was quiet for a moment, his trance like gaze fixed on the print before him.

"Now we know the sister's name," she said, "and that her husband Thomas died in the war."

"Do you have your family chart handy?"

Kate reached into her bag again and pulled out the large pad that had the beginnings of the Cheyne family tree on it. Kate added Connor's sisters name as Hannah and Thomas her husband to the chart.

Then reality of the situation returned as she fingered the two remaining letters. "What shall we do about the police?"

"It's your house that was broken into so you have to make that decision. I'm just not sure what we would tell them or what they could do about it."

Kate nodded in agreement, "It would be a little awkward especially if I told them a package was stolen that I had illegally kept and opened." Kate looked around the living room. She wondered if the thief would come back.

Birdie seemed to be reading her thoughts, "Are you alright staying here tonight by yourself?"

Kate had forgotten that her front-door lock would not be able to work properly after being forced open and now she had second thoughts about being alone.

Birdie noticed her glance at the door. He put his arm around her and held her for a moment. "If you like, I could sleep on the couch tonight. We can get a new lock tomorrow."

Kate returned the hug, "I'd feel safer, thank you."

Birdie checked his watch, "I'll be back before ten." While Birdie was picking up a few things for the night Kate got the linens for the couch ready.

Luckily she had spare sheets and pillows. Once she thought she heard a noise at the front door but when she looked it was only the screen door settling into its place.

Birdie hadn't gone far, maybe a ten minute drive from her place and it was shortly after that he arrived back, overnight bag in hand. He knocked first making sure Kate heard him before he entered then smiled at the preparations Kate was making for him. He reached into his duffle bag and pulled out something Kate had never seen before. "This should keep you safe. It's a door jam. I take it everywhere I go."

Birdie demonstrated how it was positioned against the bottom edge of the door once it was closed. It looked like a wedge and had a spike at one end that rested on the floor surface which would prevent the door from opening. "There's only one downside," he explained, "if someone forces the door then it marks the floor or carpet, but I think it should keep you safe until tomorrow." Birdie smiled at the fascination on Kate's face and handed her the door jam, "For your room, Milady." She glanced at the front door as if suggesting he use the device there. "Not to worry, if I'm set upon during the night I shall call to you frantically to telephone the police." Kate laughed at that and could just picture Birdie fighting off intruders amid bed sheets and blankets.

"It's still early, what about a snack, then we can look at the last of the letters." Kate didn't have to ask twice and quickly came back with pound cake and the remainder of white wine she had left in the refrigerator. They sat companionably for a while, each in thought over recent events while enjoying their snack.

Finished first, Kate picked up the next letter and sat closer to Birdie so that they could both see it. This letter like the last had been opened and was address to a convalescent home in southern England. It was written July, 1944.

*My Dearest Connor,*

*Spring has at last arrived. The garden tulips are more beautiful than I have seen in many years, hopefully an omen that the world will soon come to its senses and war will be a thing of the past.*

*Your letter arrived in the post this morning. I am so relieved and happy that you are recovering. For myself I am happy to hear the news of your engagement. I am most pleased you have found such a wonderful person. I hope I shall have the pleasure of meeting her before she returns to Canada.*

*Your father is of a different opinion though, as your letter has deeply angered him. He is furious and forbids you to marry a nurse and if you persist, he refuses to accept her into our family. Lord William is making it difficult for your father. Alice is his only daughter and she is devastated upon hearing of your news. She has been faithfully waiting for you to return home and has confided to me that she wishes to come and see you and persuade you to change your mind. Her father would not permit such a display and keeps her safely under watch.*

*I have always hoped you would be married in your home with your family around you but I understand your decision. An arranged marriage can not compete with love. You have been at war for so long and all I want now is your happiness. Please know that I love you and whatever you decide I will support your decision.*

*Your loving mother.*

Kate looked at Birdie, disbelief showing on her face, "Wow, what a soap opera this would make."

"It does look complicated," agreed Birdie. "So let's see what we've got." He looked at the letter again, re-reading it carefully. "It seems that Connor went against his father's wishes and married a Canadian nurse. I suppose that even in the 1940s marriages were somewhat arranged taking into account wealth and status."

"He must have met her while he was in the hospital recovering," added Kate.

"He came to Canada shortly after the war, so no marriage certificate there."

"If, they got married in Canada. What if they got married in England, then came to Canada, didn't you say their records go to 1983?"

Birdie checked the date on the letter again," Very good, my little detective, it means we need to check from May 1944 to December 1950, which is when they probably lived here."

"How do we do that?"

"We go on the Internet and check the British civil registration for those years. It will take us a while because you don't check for the exact name." Kate looked puzzled. "Each year is divided into four quarters, January to March, April to June and so forth. We type in the name Cheyne and then a list will come up for the years we want, showing the quarters for each. We go through each quarter hunting under the C's looking for the name Cheyne, then see if there is a Connor listed. If we're lucky it will show his wife's surname as well, and maybe we could find her people here in Canada. I think after 1922 they started to add that extra fact." Birdie seemed pleased with himself after a look of bewildered amazement formed on Kate's face. Now there was a chance they might find a marriage, then on second thought, "It sounds like a lengthy venture, maybe we should look at the last letter before trying the computer."

"First I think I'll open up another bottle of wine." Birdie nodded agreement and waited for Kate to rejoin him on the couch. Kate handed him a glass which had two ice cubes floating in the warm wine.

Birdie held the last letter, only unlike the other two, it was addressed to Lady Jean Cheyne. There were no stamps, yet it too was opened, which implied that it was included somehow in another letter or package that had an actual address. Kate sat close to Birdie and smiled hopefully. The letter was dated February 3 1950.

*Dear Lady Cheyne,*

*It is with deepest sorrow that I inform you of your son's death. Connor was returning home from work and was hit by a drunk driver on the highway. He died early yesterday morning of internal injuries.*

*I am shattered and lost without him. I will be leaving here soon as I cannot bear to stay longer in this house. I will take my child and go to live with my family in North Bay.*

*I am enclosing Connor's personal belongings for you to have as well as your letters to him. I know you will share my loss and I know he would want you to have these things to remember him.*

*Please let your husband know that I make no demands of him. I am sorry but this is how it must be.*

*This will be my last letter of correspondence.*

*Sincerely,*

*Anne Marie Lyonne*

Kate and Birdie just looked at the letter in silence. They had found out what they wanted to know - Connor Cheyne had married Ann Marie Lyonne, when or where didn't really seem too important. It was a sad letter and the two sat reflecting on its impact on a mother who had lost her only son so soon after the death of her husband. "I wonder why Anne Marie didn't read the letters, they were written before Connor died."

"Sometimes it takes months for a letter to come from overseas, not like today's mail." reasoned Birdie, then he smiled, "Well, maybe some surface mail."

Suddenly Kate jumped up almost knocking her glass over as her knee hit the coffee table. "He changed his name!" She paced the living room floor in her excitement. "The names on the assessment roll…Mr. and Mrs. C. Lyonne.

Then she looked at Birdie who was smiling at her exhilaration. "Wait a minute," she said, "can he do that, I mean take her name?"

"Why not, people legally change their names all the time, and they were married so instead of her changing her name he changed his. He must have had some words with his father to go to that extreme." Birdie paused for a sip of wine. "It seemed he disowned his family totally."

"That's sad." Then sitting next to Birdie again Kate reminded him about the break in. "Do you think the thief will know about the name change?"

Birdie seemed in thought, "There's no telling. It depends if Anne Marie wrote another letter to Lady Jean and it happens to be in the pile he took." With the letters gone now they would have to remember the contents from the letters they had read. He picked up the pad Kate had set on the table and began adding more information. "So we know Connor's mother was Jean and his wife was Anne Marie Lyonne, and they also had a child. "What about the phone directory?" asked Birdie, "Anne Marie might still be alive. Maybe she is still in North Bay."

"Let's check." It seemed easy enough. Check for any Anne Marie who might live in North Bay. Kate went to her computer and waited as they connected to the Internet. Once Google was up she typed in the same web site she had used to check the postal office search. Her hands trembled with excitement as she typed in the name they were hunting for. Birdie was beside her again sitting on the arm of the couch and he gave her a warm hug as the screen blinked. 'Sorry, no one by that name found' came back the response.

"Try broadening your search," he suggested.

Kate retyped the location and put in Ontario, and again was disappointed by another failure. "This time I'll leave out the first name," she said. The screen blinked back a short list of five names; a Peter Lyonne and a Y. Lyonne in Sturgeon Falls, an M. Lyonne in Niagara Falls, a V. Lyonne in Grimsby and a Simon Lyonne in Toronto. Kate made note of the names and phone numbers of the only Lyonnes found in Ontario, but she was also aware that there might be more that were unlisted numbers, but this was a start. She sat back, tired, it had been a long day.

"Here," said Birdie as he offered her, her glass. "You've done very well today."

Kate smiled a little as she turned off her computer then faced Birdie. "I guess we have if you consider Connor's family but I'm not sure we've done much that will find a relative. It seems pretty slim."

It was after eleven by the time they said their good nights. Kate had helped Birdie make up the couch and he had given her a soft kiss on the cheek in return. By one o'clock she was still awake… thinking; the days events suddenly overwhelming her. She glanced at the picture on her bedside table, then looked away as tears came to her eyes.

Kate thought she heard the telephone, it

sounded distant and muffled then she realized it was her bedside phone. Startled, she grabbed the receiver quickly so as not to wake Birdie and held it against her head as she tried to wake up. Kate could hear her name being called and finally answered in a quiet voice. “Why are you calling so early?” She checked the clock again to make sure she hadn’t misread the time. “No, I’m all right; I was out most of the day. With Birdie.” Kate half rolled over, all she wanted to do was sleep and at five-ten in the morning she decided she wasn’t in the mood for conversation. “I’ll call before lunch, okay, bye.” She hung up then slumped back into the warm covers.

# Chapter 7

The sun was filtering into her bedroom through the slats of the window blinds and suddenly she was aware of the smell of coffee. Once asleep, Kate had slept well. She was sorry she couldn't have offered Birdie better accommodations. Although her house had two bedrooms, the second one across from hers was anything but a bedroom. Fitness equipment took up most of the floor space while bookcases containing research and books lined two walls. A sewing machine on a corner table, an ironing board and two baskets of laundry completed the look.

"Good morning," came a voice from the kitchen. "Do you feel like breakfast yet?" Birdie was just pouring coffee for both of them and had a crepe pan on the stove ready to place two slices of bread now soaking in an eggy mixture. He was dressed and had a tea towel tucked into his shirt to lessen the effects of splattering bacon that he was cooking in a second pan. "I hope you don't mind," he said hesitantly, "I was up early and found some bacon in the refrigerator just begging to be cooked. It took me a while to figure out your coffee machine though."

“Well, a man who can cook. This is intriguing,” smiled Kate, secretly happy she didn’t have to cook breakfast herself.

“I have many skills,” he replied mysteriously, then turned his attention to the sizzling bacon that was almost ready to be served.

“It smells delicious, give me five minutes.”

When Kate returned, Birdie was just setting out his dishes and smiled at the look of delight on Kate’s face. Bacon, French toast and coffee greeted her as Kate sat down in her favourite chair. “This looks great!”

“Actually I had started to make bacon and scrambled eggs but then I noticed you had some maple syrup in the cupboard,” Birdie gave her a sheepish grin, “so I thought French toast would do it justice.”

“Everything looks wonderful. Wherever did you learn how to make French toast like this?” Kate cut off a portion of toast then swirled it in a puddle of maple syrup she had dribbled on to her plate. “And the bacon is perfect.” She picked up the last piece of bacon before Birdie could reach it and grinned in triumph. “I had no idea you were,” Kate paused, “so accomplished.”

He nodded in thanks while eyeing Kate as she deliberately ate the bacon slowly and sensuously. She laughed at the look on his face. “So,” she asked casually, not wanting him to know she would welcome his company again, “do you have anything planned for today?”

“Just a little renovation work then, I’m free for the day.” He started to clear away the dishes, “I’m on holidays you know. What about you? Are you going to try to find Anne Marie Lyonne?”

Kate was finishing up her coffee, “I thought I might phone a few of the numbers we found last night and see what happens, maybe we’ll find a relative.”

Birdie waited on Kate then even did the tidying up while she went and got ready for the day. He was folding up his bedding when Kate rejoined him in the living room. “Thank you for a lovely breakfast.” She helped him fold the larger blanket, “And thank you for staying over. It made me feel a lot safer.”

Birdie moved closer for the blanket’s final fold then leaned in crushing the blanket between them. His arms held her close as he gave her a gentle hug, his lips brushed against her cheek then found her lips in a warm passionate kiss. He smiled softly, his brown eyes searching hers, “You’re welcome. I’ll leave you the door jam until we fix the lock.” With that he gathered together his few belongings and prepared to leave. He showed Kate again how to use the safety device. "I'll go to the store on my way back to the flat," he checked his watch. "Do you suppose they will be open now?" It was shortly after nine so Kate gave him the directions to the nearest hardware store knowing it usually opened at eight. Birdie sized up the kind of lock he was going to need then said his farewells with a hug promising to call her when he got back to Geoffrey's. The early morning sun was shining in a blue sky giving the promise of a beautiful day.

Kate stood at the door and watched as Birdie got into his car then did as he said and placed the door wedge back in its place. She wondered if Mr. Whitmore was up and saw Birdie's car leaving at this early hour.

Birdie watched as Kate closed her door. He started the car then turned the air conditioner down a fraction from yesterday's setting and reached for his seat belt but before fastening it he reached into his jeans pocket and pulled out a gold ring. He smiled when he saw it then placed it in his jacket vest pocket.

Kate helped herself to another cup of coffee while she waited for the ringing phone to be answered. "Hi Ted," she sat down on her couch readying herself for a lengthy conversation with her sister, though more likely it would be an interrogation, "is Kelly around? Thanks."

Kelly was eager to talk to her sister and was near by when Ted answered. "So what have you been up to?" she asked accusingly. "I've been trying to reach you and every time I called I got a busy signal or no answer. You couldn't have been on the computer
at two in the morning."

"I was off the computer by ten-thirty," Kate answered, then thought a moment. She couldn't have left the computer on because she wouldn't have been able to call out now. "Maybe you miss dialed."

"You're on speed dial," argued Kelly, "that's why I called you early this morning." Kelly had calmed down somewhat, now that she had reached her sister. "Anyway, you're okay, so what's been happening?"

Kate proceeded to fill her in from the last time they had talked after the supper at the restaurant. Then something occurred to her, "Kel, how long have you known Geoffrey?" She could hear Ted in the background after Kelly had called to him with the question.

Kate heard the hesitation in Kelly's voice as she confirmed, just nine days. "You would trust a stranger who is the best friend of a virtual stranger?" Kate asked accusingly. "What if Geoffrey is some kind of nut case or thief or something worse?"

"I'm sure he's nothing of the kind," said Kelly trying to reassure her sister, then to defend her point she added, "Geoffrey is a very good photographer and has several impressive credentials." She paused, waiting for a reply that didn't come, "Besides didn't you say you liked Birdie."

Kate had said that but now there were nagging thoughts, and now the line being busy at two in the morning… Kate had written too many mystery novels to let that go unnoticed. Then again maybe it was knocked off the hook, it was right beside the makeshift bed and Birdie could easily have jolted the receiver.

"So are you going to spend the day together again?" asked Kelly. Kate could tell that she was thrilled that the blind date had been successful.

"I'm not sure yet," answered Kate, though admittedly she would love to spend more time with Birdie, "I'll wait 'till he comes back wi…er….and see what happens." Kate decided it would be better not to tell her sister about the lock or the missing package. In the mean time she had some phoning to do. "Don't worry, I'll try to call you tomorrow. Okay, bye."

Kate took the last sip of her coffee then hunted for the paper where she had written down the Lyonne phone numbers. But first she dialed zero and waited for the operator to respond. "Thank you, yes," said Kate. "Can you tell me if someone placed a long distance call using my phone early this morning?" Kate expected the operator to search the records then offer the results of her search but instead the operator told her that she could not give out that information. When Kate had asked how she would know if someone used her phone the operator explained that she would need a police search order or she could wait until she received her phone bill in the mail which would itemize any long distance calls made that month. "Thank you, anyway," replied Kate, confused yet relieved at the same time.

Kate looked at the list of Lyonne names she had jotted down last night and decided to start with the closest one living in Niagara Falls. Before dialing Kate took a moment to think about what she would say then made a couple of notes. The phone was ringing at the home of M. Lyonne, but there was no answer. After four rings the answering machine came on and Kate hung up. For something like this Kate would prefer to speak with the person, so she went on to the next number, a V. Lyonne in Grimsby.

A woman answered, "Hello," Kate said, "I'm looking for a relative of Anne Marie Lyonne who may be around eighty years old now." The woman was pleasant but offered nothing that would imply she knew of the person Kate was looking for. Whether or not Anne Marie was part of her late husband's family she had no way of knowing.

Kate crossed off the V. Lyonne on her list then as an after thought wrote husband is dead in brackets. Next was the Simon Lyonne in Toronto. A woman answered. There was a baby crying in the background and Kate suddenly had the feeling she was interrupting the woman who hurriedly asked what she wanted. The woman sounded young and called for her husband to come to the phone after Kate had asked to speak with Simon Lyonne. The man sounded gruff and answered the phone with a, "Ya, wha' d'you want?"

Kate quickly explained why she was calling and was received with a brusque, "Don't know anyone by that name," after which the receiver landed with a thump. Kate hung up, a little shaken. She crossed off the Simon Lyonne on her list and made another notation beside the name. That left two on the list both in Sturgeon Falls. Kate prepared herself for another possible hostile call and checked the area code before dialing.

Suddenly her phone rang startling her, "Hello?" It was Birdie and he was on his way back with the lock and a few of Geoffrey's tools that he would need for the installation. It would be lunch time soon so Kate decided to wait on the phone call and start to prepare a nice lunch for the two of them. Kate was excited about Birdie's return. She imagined again their early morning kiss, his muscular arms as he held her close, his moustache that thinly hugged the curve of his upper lip, the softness of his lips on hers. She felt a small shudder travel down her body then smiled to herself.

It wasn't long before the doorbell rang and Kate ran to remove the burglar device before opening the door. Birdie stood there looking like a repair man. He had on his jeans, an old plaid shirt and a paint splashed baseball cap that he wore low shading his eyes. He carried what must have been Geoffrey's tool box in one hand and a package from the hardware store in the other which he proudly handed to Kate. "No one's going to get past this!" he announced. "I decided to get a deadbolt lock."

Kate took the package from him as Birdie sat down the tool box. She took out the box containing the lock and looked at the attached receipt. "I should have this much in my purse," she said, intending to reimburse Birdie for his purchase.

"That's quite alright, let's call it even." He gave Kate a warm hug. "I hope you don't mind, but I used your phone last night to call home. I wanted to talk to my sister before she went to work."

Kate smiled and was happy now that the

phone call question had been resolved. He took the lock from Kate and opened the box. "Do you know how to do this?" she asked giving him a dubious look.

"It looks simple enough," he fished out a piece of paper from the bottom of the box, "and it comes with instructions."

"Wow, you are an exceptional man," then she laughed, "I'll bet you stop and ask for directions too."

"Only, if I'm lost." He opened the tool box and took out the chisel and drill he would need.

"I have a snack almost ready." Seeing his reaction to the mention of food, Kate smiled, "I'll go and put on the tea."

Birdie prepared to install the new lock. He waved at Mr. Whitmore across the street. It was a warm sunny day, the same kind of day he found out about young Alexander Cheyne. Alex hadn't been difficult to get close to. A boozer and a gambler, Birdie had found him late one night in a local gentlemen's club.

Alexander had just received the letter and was acutely aware of how precarious his position was. The letter he confessed had been accusing, implying his great grandfather had stolen Connor Cheyne's birth right and it declared there was an heir to the estate living in Canada.

Written by Connor's mother, the letter was

convincing and Alexander had been afraid. He had to find out if there was any truth to it. Could his potential fortune be snapped away from him? He had contacted the family lawyer and now finally knew the truth to the fifty-year clause in his Great, Great, Grandfather's will. He was in a panic, and under the influence of drink had easily bonded with the young man who sat next to him who claimed to be a detective and for a fee, offered to help keep the secret. Together they planned that Robin Nightingale would go to Canada and try to trace any possible heir then stall any possible claim to the family fortune.

That had been eleven days ago and now Birdie sat wondering if he should confess his deception. He had wanted to spend some time with Kate and in doing so had perpetuated the lie that he was on holidays. Would she understand? He looked at the tool box that he had borrowed from the Holiday Inn caretaker along with his cap and felt ashamed. He could probably continue the search on his own and just not contact Kate again but something about her drew him and he couldn't let go yet.

Kate called from the kitchen.

"Almost done," he answered.

Kate joined him then assessed the job. "Very good," she said, glad now that she wouldn't have to worry about her next night alone in her house.

"It won't be easy to get past this lock," then he demonstrated the locks unique qualities.

Kate smiled as she saw his enthusiasm. He had some black grease from the lock on his hand and a smudge on his face. "Here." She said, and taking her hand towel wiped the mark from his face. His brown eyes followed hers and he smiled back, glad now that he was here with her.

"Maybe I should go and tidy up."

They enjoyed a light lunch of cucumber slices and toasted tuna salad sandwiches and tea of course. Kate filled Birdie in regarding her phone calls to the various Lyonne numbers. "That leaves just two." Kate suddenly looked concerned. "What happens if we don't find a relative?"

"Well, I suppose you could check all the Lyonnes in Canada, maybe someone might be a relative, but I'm sure that would take a while and probably be quite expensive."

"Oh, I forgot! There's one in Niagara Falls. I'll try again now!" Leaving her last half of sandwich with a small nibble in its side Kate went back to her phone and dialed the Niagara Falls number that she had written on a scratch pad next to the phone. The phone rang four times then an answering machine kicked in with the usual request.

This time Kate left a message. "Hi, my name

is Kate. I'm looking for a relative of Anne Marie Lyonne who may have lived in North Bay." Kate then left her number along with the date and time. "There," she said, "now two more to go."

Birdie finished his last bite of sandwich then joined Kate in the living room, tea in hand. She looked at him hopefully as she dialed the long distance number to Y. Lyonne in Sturgeon Falls.

"Hello, I'm calling regarding Anne Marie Lyonne who lived in North Bay. I was hoping you might be a relative." Kate's eyes hadn't left Birdie the entire time she was speaking. The woman on the other end sounded older and seemed not to mind a call from a complete stranger. Many people anticipating a sales pitch from a telemarketer wouldn't have stayed on the line to hear Kate's explanation. "You are!" Kate smiled and gave Birdie an enthusiastic nod. "I have a package that belongs to her husband and was hoping you might know…" Kate paused, "Oh, I'm sorry to hear that." Her expression changed now and Birdie could only guess the result. Anne Marie was no longer alive.

"What about her son?" Kate continued, hoping to get a positive reply, "I could probably give the package to him." She waited. "War mementoes, letters, photos of the family and some jewellery." Kate listened patiently as the woman explained she was a niece of Anne Marie who had lived with her family for a short while in North Bay. Anne Marie had died suddenly four years after her husband of a burst appendix and the young son William had been raised by his mother's brother Pierre. Kate now had the name of Connor's son and felt her search narrowing. Will moved away from that area when he was eighteen hoping to gain employment in Toronto was all she knew.

By her defeated expression Birdie knew the results of her inquiry lead to a dead end. Quickly Birdie scrawled a word on the scratch pad next to Kate. Kate glanced down, searched Birdie's face for a moment then, nodded. "I believe Will might be heir to an estate in Scotland. Is there anything else you can remember that might help me locate him?"

At this news the woman hesitated then added, "There might be someone else who could help you. Will had a good friend years ago, Frank Stone." She went on to explain that usually Frank came north to stay for a few days with his mother. Luckily Frank would be arriving early tomorrow morning to stay for a week or two.

"Do you think he would speak with us if we came up tomorrow?" Kate glanced excitedly at Birdie. "27 Mason Street…after nine o'clock. Thank you." Kate hung up the phone then collapsed on the couch beside Birdie, a huge grin on her face.

"What luck!"

Birdie sat contentedly on the edge of his seat as Kate explained. "That lady was Yvonne Lyonne. Her father and Anne Marie were brother and sister. Anne Marie went to live with Yvonne's parents in North Bay. After she died, Will, as she called him went to live with another of Anne Marie's brothers in Sturgeon Falls. Then around eighteen he left and she thinks he moved to Toronto."

"An old friend is arriving tomorrow who would possibly know where he is…and." Kate was so excited she almost forgot to take a breath, "she said if we come by her place after nine we might talk to him about Will." Kate was so happy, glad now that she had taken a chance and opened the package. Then she looked at Birdie, a questioning look crossed her face. "Why did you think William might be an heir to an estate?"

He'd realized his slip as soon as he had suggested this tact with his note but couldn't think of anything immediate other than a weak excuse, "It seemed like it might be a possibility, especially what we know about Connor's Uncle. Besides we found someone who is a relative and we have an invitation." He hoped this explanation although not totally untrue was sufficient.

Birdie looked at her expectantly, “Am I invited.”

Kate gave him a hug, “Of course you are,” then added, “but, only if I pay the expenses.”

Birdie was about to protest then saw the look of determination on Kate’s face and he surrendered gracefully. “Then I accept. I suppose we should leave quite early tomorrow morning.”

“Wait a minute!” Kate suddenly thought of something they had both had forgotten, “We don’t have the package anymore! She’s going to expect the things I’ve mentioned over the phone.”

“We’ll just have to be honest and tell her what really happened.”

Kate nodded, “I guess so, there’s not much else we can do. At least we have a few letters to show her. Kate gave Birdie an excited grin. “Why don’t we leave this afternoon. I can find us a place to stay then we can be at her place just after nine without having to get up so early.”

“This promises to be an interesting holiday.” Birdie was readying himself to leave in preparation for their trip. “What time do you want to leave?”

“Around five should get us past the Toronto rush hour traffic,” Kate knew that the peak hours were between one and five o’clock, so if they left at five they would hit Toronto around six-thirty hopefully avoiding the traffic jams and delays.

"Then I shall need to collect a few things from the flat." Kate's mood was infectious and Birdie laughed to himself. "This is truly remarkable," he said, "one minute I'm visiting an old friend then the next I'm off on an adventure into the wilds of northern Canada."

The look on his face reminded her of a small boy who'd just discovered his favourite candy sitting on the kitchen table, "Well, it's more like central Ontario and it's not totally wild but it is an adventure and I can't wait."

# Chapter 8

After a hug and kiss on the cheek goodbye, Birdie left, leaving Kate alone with her thoughts on the front step of her house.

Mr. Whitmore was just leaving his porch readying himself for an hour or two of gardening work. He waved when he saw Kate, Birdie's leaving having attracted his attention.

Kate rushed over. She was dying to share her news. She caught up to Mr. Whitmore by the small wooden garden shed he had built almost fifty years ago. The green wooden screen door had recently been replaced but the flat vertical boards of the building looked ragged and uneven around the perimeter of the structure.

"You look as if you have some good news," he commented when he saw Kate's excited grin.

"We found a relative of the wife who lived across the street." Kate went on to explain the name change, her people up north, her son and the possible chance of finding out his whereabouts in Sturgeon Falls.

"My, you have been busy." His tools were all

lined up on the side of a counter just inside the door. Mr. Whitmore took the spade and weed poker that Kate offered him. "I'll keep an eye on your place while you're gone. Will your car be in the driveway?"

Kate guessed this was Mr. Whitmore's subtle way of asking if Birdie was going along with her.

Kate smiled. "I haven't had it fixed yet and it's a little too risky to take on a long trip, so Birdie's driving."

He smiled back, "I'm glad you're not going alone, I like that young man."

Kate put her arm around his shoulders and gave him a warm hug, "Well, I better go now. I've got to look on the computer for some rooms near Sturgeon Falls."

"Let me know how you make out," was Mr. Whitmore's farewell.

Kate was still on the computer when Birdie arrived back, case in hand and grinning like a school boy ready for a great adventure. It had taken Kate a while to find accommodations during this peak summer time when most lodges were booked solid. She had contemplated a roadside motel but had finally found a lodge on Lake Nippissing which had an apartment available for the weekend after a late cancellation.

Toronto traffic was bearable, packed with vehicles by the time they got to the Oakville area, an accident having caused a backup an hour earlier. Thankfully the traffic kept moving and even fifty kilometers an hour was preferable to being stuck in a parking lot scenario which Kate had witnessed on several occasions before during rush hour.

Birdie drove and it was now that Kate relaxed and took the time to notice this tall British stranger for whom she was developing a fondness. He wore jeans and a blue plaid shirt unbuttoned at the neck with the long sleeves rolled up. It seemed to Kate that he hadn't stopped smiling, so eager for this chance to see and do more in a country he had until now only just read about.

When Kate had told Birdie they were staying at a lodge he questioned her about every aspect of lodge life. 'Were there boats for hire? Could fishing trips be arranged? Did he need a license?' Kate doubted there would be time to indulge in vacation behaviour but she dutifully answered all of his questions about northern life.

Kate checked her on route itinerary that she had printed after consulting Map Quest on her computer. She was familiar with the roads north of Toronto yet had not heard of this particular lodge before so once past Orillia she checked to make sure they were on the right road.

It was close to eight o'clock when Kate noticed him. He was driving a two door Explorer with a rental license plate. Kate was sure they had passed him during the delay at Oakville because he had eyed Kate sitting in the passenger seat as traffic slowed, and now here he was again as they both took the same road north. He could have been a vacationer going north just as they were but Kate still kept a watchful eye.

Birdie was enjoying the view. Living in a big city was nothing new to him but once they had left cities behind and entered the cottage country with its abundant lakes many of which could be seen from the highway, Birdie was overwhelmed by the vastness of it all. Numerous times he had Kate pull out the Ontario map from the side-door pocket and he glanced in wonderment as Kate kept track of their journey with a highlight marker.

"Back home you can cross the whole country from sea to sea in five hours, but here you're still in the same province after driving, what twelve hours?" he looked to Kate for a nod in agreement.

Kate hadn't mentioned it before but the thought of who had the package contents now, and why, worried her.

"Who do you think stole the package?"

Birdie was eyeing a service centre up ahead and knew they could both use a break. He signaled his intention to turn as they eased into the exit lane. "I don't know, but there must be more to it than we're aware of or else why risk breaking into a house for a few mementoes."

"And how did he know I had the package in the first place?" added Kate.

Birdie thought about Geoffrey out west right now. Geoffrey, a rogue in his own right usually carried documents and credentials ready for all and any eventuality. They had arranged for Geoffrey to steal the package and thus leave Kate free from the investigation but once having met her, Birdie had phoned his colleague and changed the plan.

It was Geoffrey who had arrived in the country earlier and had checked out the address he was given for the package. It hadn't taken him long to investigate the writer who lived at the address. Kate's publisher had been easy to convince when Geoffrey pretended to be an old friend of Kate's sister claiming she had married and he didn't know how to contact her. He was glad the publisher hadn't thought to suggest he contact Kate directly and ask her himself.

Once finding out about the sister and her husband, Geoffrey was able to fit into the company requirements. Ted was an easy going sort of person and upon over hearing a conversation between he and his wife regarding Kelly's younger sister, Geoffrey had revised his plan and confided in Ted that he was looking for a date for his visiting British friend. It didn't take long for the two to win over the naive couple.

And now Geoffrey was in Vancouver and Birdie was traveling with a woman he had just met into the wilds of Canada. Like Kate, he had wondered who had stolen the package, had Alex Cheyne hired another detective, and if so, why?

Signs alerted travelers when a service centre was available and now Birdie was preparing to stop and take a long needed break. The food and beverage building was adjacent to three lines of gas pumps. Birdie found a spot not far from one of the building's two entrances and pulled up beside a vacationing family in a long van. A black Explorer followed suit and pulled into the next vacant space behind and to their left. Kate noticed him when she turned to retrieve her bag from the back seat. "That truck, he's been following us since Oakville." Kate turned back without looking directly at the driver.

Birdie glanced nonchalantly into his side mirror. "Actually he started to follow us as soon as we left your street." He saw Kate's look of alarm.

"He may be the man who broke into your house."

Kate remembered looking at him as he had passed their car at Oakville. He had had long stringy blonde hair and a scruffy unshaven appearance. She remembered how he had smiled at her when passing. Kate resisted the urge to turn around and look at the driver again. "We can't let him follow us."

"I know." Birdie turned to look at her. "We need some way to stop him."

"He's going to wonder why we are just sitting here." Kate opened her door as if preparing to go inside. "Walk with me to the entrance and we'll see what he does. He probably needs gas too and a washroom break." Kate noticed Birdie's puzzled look, "Petrol and toilet," she clarified.

Birdie smiled back.

Together they walked to the side entrance. At one point Kate dropped her bag so she could turn around while she picked it up. "He's still sitting in the truck."

They decided to order from the chicken fast food booth and once their food was deposited on their tray Kate led Birdie to a vacant table near the window. Almost forgetting their situation Birdie was delighted with the amount of food Kate had ordered. Chicken fingers, fries, onion rings, and a cola crowded his side of the tray.

"What about putting water in his gas tank?" suggested Kate.

Birdie finished squeezing the envelope of plum sauce onto his plate before answering. "We'd need something with a nozzle and a fair amount of water."

Kate reached into her bag and pulled out a half filled bottle of soda water.

"It might work," agreed Birdie, "but it wouldn't stop his car straight away. I'd rather flatten his tires first then we could add the water." He devoured an onion ring before continuing, "Either way we'd have to get him away from the truck first."

Kate slid the remainder of her fries out of their container onto a paper napkin then proceeded to undo the end then roll up the cardboard into a cylinder. She smiled at her resourcefulness, "A funnel!" She got up abruptly then went over to the condiment section of the eating area and came back with a handful of small packets. "We might as well sweeten things up a bit for him." Kate then tore open the small sugar packages and poured their contents into the bottle of soda water watching it fizz a little as she replaced the cap.

"You better add one packet of mustard for colouring," suggested Birdie. "That way if anyone sees me, I can pretend I'm putting in petrol."

Obediently Kate got up and returned with a packet of mustard.

Birdie was on the window facing side of the table and saw now that the driver was out and walking up to the same entrance they had just used. Their table was between the two entrances across from the food booths behind them. He was getting closer and there wasn't much time. "When he comes in, try to get in front of him in line, then order some more food but try to stall. I'll get up as he gets nearer and say I need to use the 'washroom'." He set the bottle of soda water next to the seat in front of him as he got up and explained his leaving the table. The unsuspecting driver passed by Birdie who suggested loud enough for him to hear that Kate go and get another order of fries and onion rings.

Kate paused just long enough for her to determine which line the driver would approach then quickly moved to get a spot in front of him. While he was reading the menu selections a young man with a small son stepped in line behind Kate. Birdie left the table hugging the soda water bottle in front of him.

The vehicles couldn't be observed from the take out lines so he had to work quickly before the driver either sat down at a table or came out with his food.

It wasn't difficult. Luckily the gas tank wasn't

the kind that locked and it was on the hidden side of the truck. Birdie fitted the cylinder into the tank opening and proceeded to pour in the bottle's contents. The father of the family in the van next to them gave him a curious look as Birdie was pouring the light-coloured liquid into the tank. Birdie shook his head and smiled, "This is filling up the hard way," he said, "but it'll be enough to get me over to the pumps." The man smiled back then went on his way.

It didn't take long. Birdie glanced past the truck to check their table by the window. No Kate, so there was still time. He crouched down pretending to tie his shoes and at the same time reached in his pocket for a tool that he often kept for such occasions. Looking like a miniature ice pick with a wooden handle, it went easily into the tire wall, which made a hissing sound as the air escaped. It felt like a lifetime, but finally it was flat. He checked again as Kate was just sitting down at the table. He moved backwards crouching to the front tire, out of view of the window and repeated the operation until he heard the hissing sound of air.

Once at the front he could stand up without being seen. He glanced into the front seat of the truck and saw a familiar package, luckily the driver had left the door unlocked. Resuming his crouching position Birdie moved back to the driver's door. He had to be quick. The package was neatly folded which made it easier to grab. Once he had retrieved the brown paper wrapping with its small bundles secured, Birdie went past the front of the truck back to his own vehicle and opened the door.

Kate was back at her seat now watching anxiously as the driver went out the door and walked down the concrete path back toward his truck. Quickly Birdie started his car and pulled forward. He turned as if to leave the parking lot causing the driver to abruptly stop and look, then turned again and drove to the far side of the service centre towards the building's second entrance. Kate immediately got up and ran to the alternate door. This side of the building was higher up and there were a lengthy number of decorative winding steps to descend before she reached the car.

Birdie was smiling as she rushed to get inside.

"That was great!" she gasped, enjoying the intrigue of it all. "Did you have any problems?"

Birdie smiled as he thought about the driver. He wished he could have seen the look on his face. Then he glanced back into the back seat. "I have a present for you."

Kate turned to see what it was and immediately recognized the stolen package lying open with its contents spread out on the seat. "So, we were right!" she exclaimed. "I wonder if everything's here?"

"We still need petrol," reminded Birdie. "We can reach the pumping area from this side." He followed the winding road around the service centre approaching the pumps from the other side. Birdie pulled up to the first empty area not wanting to pull too far forward in case he could be seen by the driver of the black truck. There was a small store attached to the gas pump area selling everything that a traveler could possibly need on the road.

The pumps were an older type that didn't allow you to swipe your credit card at the pump so after filling up Kate went inside to pay. Once back at the car Birdie decided to quickly check out the store and left Kate to keep watch while he went inside. An impatient woman driver pulled up behind Kate and honked several times for her to pull forward before backing up then going around to the first pump. She gave Kate an aggravated look as she passed.

A phone suddenly rang a familiar melody from Carmen. It took Kate a moment to find the cell phone in the car's glove compartment. She hesitated, then looked toward the store. There was no sign of Birdie so Kate flipped open the case and answered. She felt someone was there but there was no reply. Then she heard a voice talking to someone in the distance and could hear sounds of traffic in the background. Kate said 'Hello' again then the party hung up. She closed the lid and set the phone in the console area next to her.

Birdie came out of the store carrying a bag and smiling. "I thought we might like a snack since we didn't get to eat much of our meal." He handed the bag to Kate. Chocolate bars of various descriptions occupied the contents. Birdie noticed his cell phone resting in the console.

"Someone called," Kate explained, "I hope you don't mind."

"Not at all." Birdie backed the car up and prepared to leave the service area from the far exit. "Who was it?"

"I don't know, maybe it was a wrong number. Two people were talking. They listened for a while before hanging up."

Birdie glanced down and retrieved his phone. He stopped the car so he could check the incoming numbers then smiled, "Just Geoffrey. Probably wondering how I'm making out without him." He set the phone down then followed a gray van out on to the highway. Kate checked her watch, it was just after six o'clock and they were once again back on the road north to Sturgeon Falls.

"We should have a good twenty minute lead

on our black-truck friend, that is if he gets it going." Birdie smiled at their cunning.

"When do you expect Geoffrey back?" she asked, trying to sound casual.

"I should think he'd be finished the job by Wednesday or Thursday." Birdie glanced over and gave Kate a reassuring smile. "It's too bad he's not here with us, I'm sure he would enjoy the hunt we're on. But then on the other hand, Geoffrey is rather a hit with the ladies so I'm just as glad he's in Vancouver." Then switching the topic he asked. "How far do we go on this highway?"

Kate abandoned her thoughts about Geoffrey for the moment and reached for her map. "A few more hours." she said, "Once we get to North Bay it's not far to the lodge."

Kate spent the next few miles thinking about the driver in the black truck…why was he following them…and who was he working for? Who was this man she was heading north with? If she was writing this story herself she would have the driver working for Birdie as he accompanied the poor unsuspecting heroine in search of yet another clue. But what was so important about Connor Cheyne? Okay, fifty years ago there was an estate at stake but surely by now that had been resolved. Why was the package so important?

Her thoughts were broken by Birdie rummaging through the plastic bag that sat on the console, hunting for a chocolate bar. “I’m starting to get rather hungry.”

“Here, you drive, I’ll do that.” Kate pulled out four bars and then gave him a smile. “How about the one with fudge and nuts?”

“Sounds delicious.” He licked his lips in exaggerated anticipation while Kate peeled back the wrapper and handed him the prepared chocolate bar. Birdie smiled his thanks and prepared to devour the bar.

He looked almost boyish as he bit off a huge piece. Kate watched as he drove. She thought about the first time they had met, their time together at the beach, their first kiss. She had started to care for this stranger and she wanted so much to believe in him, but something wasn’t right…she wasn’t sure what it was but it nagged at her just the same.

The sign for highway seventeen was up ahead. It was time to turn off highway eleven and take the westerly cutoff towards North Bay. It took another forty minutes for the two to reach Beaver Tail Lodge.

The lodge itself consisted of eight housekeeping cottages scattered among tall pines and birch trees and eight apartments that lined two floors next to the main building which housed the kitchen, dining room, store and communal living room with stone fireplace.

Kate had booked their last available room on the upper floor and was glad when the owner had described the room as having two queen sized beds and a private bath. The apartments were long and narrow with a small bedroom to their left as they entered. A bathroom and dressing area lined the hallway which opened up into a living room with kitchenette area. There was a small screened-in deck that overlooked Lake Nippissing. Kate paused at the bedroom door then realized the couch must also be a pull out bed.

Birdie was pleased with the accommodations. Eagerly Kate set the package down on the fifties style metal kitchen table by the window. Everything seemed to be as it had been in her house, everything except the ring. That was gone, probably lost during the packages back and forth travels or kept by its thief.

Birdie was enjoying the view. Their room overlooked a small beach area where young children swam and played while their mothers kept a watchful eye. Next to the beach and nestled in behind a man-made gravel island was the docking area. Its lack of boats told Kate that many were already out on the lake enjoying the evenings fishing. This evening promised to be beautiful bringing a quiet and calmness to the lake. The sky in the west was beginning to show the colourful shades of pink and orange that reflected onto the few fluffy clouds that rested above the horizon. She remembered many such nights as a child. Kelly always wanted to swim or water ski while she and her father enjoyed the stillness of the lake fishing.

Birdie had found a comfortable chair on the deck and seemed content to watch and wait for the sunset that promised to be spectacular, that is until Kate mentioned supper. Luckily Kate had thought to reserve supper as well as their room after speaking with the owner. Although they had arrived a little later than planned Kate found the owner very obliging.

The dining room was almost empty by the time they came downstairs. Cottagers usually liked to stay out until dark, fishing for that ultimate catch, so most lodges scheduled their evening meal for five or six which left time for fishing after. Some like this one offered a later meal time and kept an open dining room up until nine then a reduced menu of finger foods until ten.

While waiting for their meal Kate asked the waitress if she knew how to get to Mason Street in Sturgeon Falls. Luckily she knew the area and Kate carefully took down the directions.

The dining room was decorated with a log cabin motif. Pine panels hugged the walls in a horizontal fashion, while stuffed fish and mounted heads of various north land creatures watched over the diners as they ate.

Birdie looked tired. They had driven with just the one stop and now he was ready to relax. He fussed with his napkin then moved his cutlery as the waitress served him his dish. "I can't wait until tomorrow. Do you think we'll have some time to go out on the lake?"

Kate waited as her dish was being served before answering. "Maybe. If we get up real early we could go out before meeting Ms. Lyonne." She cut up her breaded whitefish before adding a dash of vinegar. "We should go through the letters though, just in case she wants them." In theory though they had accomplished their purpose of finding a relative of Connor Cheyne's family, they didn't really need to search further. "I know we don't need to but I'm curious. We've gotten to know Connor and …I just wonder if there is more to his story."

Birdie nodded in agreement, his mouth full of grilled steak as the waitress came by with the bottle of white wine Kate had ordered. She smiled at Birdie. "You do love your food, don't you?"

"I love good food, I love beautiful surroundings and I love beautiful women." With that he raised his glass, "To Connor Cheyne, the man who brought us together."

"To Connor Cheyne," she said warmly.

They were enjoying the last of their dessert when suddenly Birdie looked very serious. He looked into Kate's eyes and seemed saddened by something. "There's something I need to tell you," he started, a little hesitant. "I should have told you from the beginning but I didn't know how." He paused tentative, knowing now that what he would say would hurt her. He refilled their glasses with the remainder of the wine then picked up Kate's glass. "Let's go upstairs and talk."

# Chapter 9

Kate led the way as the two went back up the stairs to the apartment. "Would you bring your chart with you?" he asked as he went straight to the deck and placed their glasses on the small plastic table that sat below the large screened window. There were two wicker chairs that Birdie moved closer together then he waited as Kate sat down, curious about this revelation.

He started slowly, looking at her as he spoke. "My name…is… Robin Nightingale, but I'm not a writer." He paused then, swallowed. He saw the look of confusion on Kate's face. "I was sent here to find a descendant of Connor Cheyne." Kate said nothing but kept her focus on him, searching his face. "Geoffrey's my accomplice." Seeing Kate was still calm and not yet angry at his deception he continued, "He found out all about you and your family before I arrived then arranged for you and I to meet."

"You lied to me!" Her eyes narrowed and she raised her hand. No, she wouldn't strike him as much as the impulse flashed through her. She'd known there was something that didn't seem right, "How could you do such a thing?" Hurt was slowly replacing the anger…she had liked him…trusted him.

"Please believe me, I am so very sorry for the deception, but once it began it suddenly seemed so difficult to tell you." Then his eyes left hers and he lowered his gaze, "I wanted to spend more time with you," he said softly, "I know that's not an excuse."

A mosquito buzzed past her ear and landed on her arm. She swatted it then flicked at the squashed body. "No, it's not," she said finally. He looked worried and his eyes showed the stress of the days driving burdened now by his confession.

Calm now, Kate picked up both glasses and handed one to Birdie. He drank half of the wine in his glass in one long gulp then put his glass back on the table. He wanted to take her in his arms…to feel the warmth of her…to hold her.

Kate thought back to their first meeting at her front door. She was calmer now and had a little sympathy for the pain he was still in. "And what would you have done if I had been an eighty-year-old widow?"

Birdie smiled at the same thought he had two weeks ago then looked into Kate's eyes. "I would have told you the truth. I would have come to your door and told you that my aged Grandmother who has Alzheimer's sent a family package to your address by mistake."

Totally confused now, Kate sat back in her chair. "So you knew what was in the package all along!" she said accusingly.

"No! Only that it contained family items and was sent in hopes of reaching Connor's family." Birdie looked hesitant; he was afraid of this and feared losing Kate's trust forever. "Let me show you," he said softly. He picked up the pad with the Cheyne family chart on the front page and started to fill in the empty spaces.

Next to the Grandfather, Birdie penciled in William Cheyne. Next to Hannah's baby he printed the name Jeanette. He made the equal sign next to Jeanette then added the name of her husband-Mark Nightingale. He drew a short vertical line below them then drew a horizontal line below it with two more vertical lines at either end to indicate two children. The first name he wrote was Alexis, the second name he wrote in slower strokes was Robin.

"Hannah…is your Grandmother!" she said slowly confirming the connection. "Why didn't you tell me the truth anyway?" she asked pleadingly. "I would have understood."

"Believe me, I regret that very much. But it seemed that once the lie got started it was too difficult to change." He set down the pad hoping to redeem himself, “I’ll answer all your questions. What would you like to know?”

For the first time since they met there was an awkward silence. Kate was quiet for a moment as she looked into Birdie’s eyes. He seemed truly sorry and hurt by his deception.

“First off,” she said, “who is Alexander Cheyne?”

Birdie picked up the pad and drew as he spoke. “Alex is, my third cousin I believe.” He filled in the name for Connor’s father printing in Michael then added the name Duncan for the Uncle. “Michael’s brother was Duncan, the bad guy in the letters. His son was James. James eventually took over the family estate, and his grandson Alex now controls the lands and money.”

“Connor’s mother Jean lived with my Grandmother for many years. Once she got the news Connor was dead she had no choice but to tell his Grandfather, William about it. Hoping one day to see Connor’s child she kept the letters, his personal things and some family history in a package, that she would one day send to him in Canada, but that day never came.”

“On her death bed she wrote a letter to Alexander Cheyne’s father Duncan. In it she told of Connor’s son in Canada and if claimed in time this rightful heir could take over everything he held as being his own."

"Unfortunately she entrusted all this to my Grandmother Hannah, who at the time was already developing signs of Alzheimer's. My Grandmother has kept the package and the letter all these years in a cupboard, forgotten, that is until three weeks ago when she found them, saw that they were addressed to her brother in Canada and a Cheyne who lived in her childhood home, then posted them." Birdie took a sip of wine before continuing, "I only found out because in one of her more lucid moments she told my mother in a fit of panic about the package and the letter, about her mother's hope and her grandfather's despair. I had heard stories about Cheyne relatives but had never met them so I went to Edinburgh. I did a little investigating on my own and found out a great deal about the Cheyne family. It wasn't hard to find Alex in one of his local haunts."

"What did Jean mean about an heir being found in time? Didn't Alex's family inherit the estate?"

"Not, exactly. After Connor's death, his Grandfather William entailed his estate and money, not wanting his wastrel son Duncan to gamble and drink away all he had worked for." Birdie set his glass down then turned to Kate seeking assurance before continuing. "After reading the letter Jean sent, Alex checked with his solicitor. Up until then he did not know about the fifty-year condition to William Cheyne's will." He saw the puzzled look on Kate's face, then further explained. "The will states that if a male descendant of Connor Cheyne is found within fifty years of William's death then he will have all rights and title to the lands, estate and money. Alex's family have been living on the estate and enjoying a generous allowance since William's death. I doubt Alex's father even knew about the condition.

"So when is the fifty years up?"

"Alex confided in me that the deadline is September fourteenth."

"So, Alex hired you to make sure that no heir could be found."

"Something like that, but I had my own reasons for seeking him out." He took another sip of wine before continuing. "I pursued this for my family. My Grandmother needs closure. Even if she doesn't remember, I will know I did all I could. If I had known about the condition in the will I would have looked into this long before now."

"So, who stole the package from my house?"

"There you've got me," said Birdie shaking his head slowly. He set down his glass next to Kate's and turned to her. "Originally I was to find out if you had the package and if so somehow retrieve it. Later Geoffrey and I…"

"But he was on his way to Vancouver," Kate interrupted.

"Yes. After I had noticed the package was opened and it seemed we might explore it together, I phoned Geoffrey later and told him not to worry about it, that I had the package and there was nothing in it to indicate an heir might be living."

She nodded slowly, trying to piece everything together, "So who exactly is Geoffrey, and how long have you known him?"

Birdie smiled, "Not long, he's an … acquaintance who has worked on a few jobs with me. He usually goes ahead and sets up the situation." Kate smiled thinking of herself as a situation.

"So it was Geoffrey you phoned from my house!"

"Yes, he was glad everything worked out so quickly and said he'd join me on Thursday." He saw Kate's train of thought shift to their present situation and read her mind, "But I don't know the man who was following us or why he stole the package."

Birdie took Kate's hands in his and pressed them tight. "I'm sorry I deceived you." He caressed her hands in his, hoping he had said enough for redemption, "Am I forgiven?"

Kate released her hands and leaned close to him. Her arms surrounded him and he pressed her nearer. "You're forgiven," she whispered. He gently kissed the soft whiteness of her neck in appreciation, then leaned back.

"There's one more thing," he said, "I found this next to your computer." With a sheepish look he presented Kate with the missing gold ring. "When I was young my Grandmother told me this was an important part of our family history and never to lose it." He pulled a second ring out of his jeans pocket and placed it back on his right hand. "I didn't know there were two rings. I was afraid you might compare them, so I hid mine."

Kate smiled, "Luckily for me that I did just that after you left." Birdie gave her a knowing look. "That's why the thief didn't find it, I'd forgotten I left it by the computer." Kate looked at the ring and placed on her third finger. She held her hand out admiringly. "I'm glad you found it." Kate suddenly felt foolish. "So you knew about Connor all along?"

"No, really, I was just as intrigued as you were by him. My mother seldom spoke of him. To her he was just the Uncle she never knew that went to the Americas. After my Grandmother became ill no one ever talked of him or the rest of the family. I never knew he came to Canada until this business with the package came up. What I learned about the Cheynes, I found out from Alex and local gossip. Alex can be very informative after a few drinks."

The sound of a boat motor caught their attention. Out on the lake, white, red and green lights betrayed the path of the last boat to come in off the lake from fishing. The boat slowed as it approached the island then stopped after it pulled into one of the furthest docks.

"Most of my family research was on my father's side." Birdies eyes brightened, "We're supposed to be related to William Wallace. I guess that's what drew me to the hunt."

Kate, her emotions calmed, looked at her friend, "Well, are you?"

Birdie laughed, "That's still to be proven, I'm only back to the eighteenth century. I suppose that's why I like my work. It involves clues and hunts for missing people."

"Didn't you know about your family's wealth in Scotland?"

"Growing up I don't remember the subject coming up. The ring was an important family memento but that's all my mother knew. Alexander Cheyne's carousing had been in the local paper once. My Grandmother received a small yearly income of her own, and my father wasn't exactly poor, so the

Cheynes weren't a part of our family that we were missing."

It was dark now and the sounds of the lake had changed from children's laughter and motors revving to sounds of water rolling up onto the beach in rhythmic waves and the occasional ghostly sound of a loon in a distant bay. It was a beautiful clear night and the stars put on a spectacular show. "I've never seen so many stars," she said.

Kate felt much better after they had talked. She believed Birdie and felt the trust return. "Shall we look at some letters?"

Kate went to get the stack of letters then rejoined Birdie on the deck. She looked at the cause of all this intrigue. The letters seemed as they were, still held in place by twine and she doubted the thief had even looked at them. Kate took their restriction off and fanned the stamped edges looking for one of the older letters and chose one near the bottom. The stamp had the likeness of Edward VII. It had several ink stamps across the front. The ink writing was heavy and had bled through the paper making the name and address barely legible. It was old and fragile worn thin by numerous readings. It was dated May 3, 1902. Birdie moved his chair closer so he could follow along as Kate read.

*My Love,*

*I hope this letter finds you well. I thank God that I have survived yet another day of fighting. The Boers have pulled back and we suffered only one casualty. We are camped now beside a small town. I have news that may change our fate forever.*

* * *

William Alexander Cheyne set his pen down. How could he tell Lydia about today. That he had killed a man, not his first in close range and not in battle but in a drunken brawl, defending himself.

The day had been long and again he felt blessed not to have been killed or worse still, wounded. A few hours rest was welcome after the torrential down pour of that day and Lieutenant Cheyne of the Cameronian Rifles, and two of his buddies had sought comfort in a local tavern.

At another table drunk and loud sat two civilians, their loyalty to the Boers obvious by their talk. They were big men, miners, and when the serving girl brought them more beer they turned on her as if it was her fault enemy soldiers were present. The girl had cried out as she was struck. The frail bartender could only watch as others in the place sided with the miners. Feeling the climate changing for the worse and strongly outnumbered, William had pulled out his revolver anticipating the outcome of their wild talk.

Jimmy and Paddy had also drawn their weapons and together, slowly the three had backed out of the tavern and into the rain soaked street again. William looked down at the cobble stoned street, shiny with the renewed rain. The rivulets of water had been rivulets of blood earlier as his company had taken over the town in an effort to find and capture a small band of retreating Boer Guerrillas. Most of the townspeople were glad the fighting was brief and their possessions safe and seemed more than welcoming as the British moved in knowing that as soon as they left their guerrilla forces would retake the area. Tired, the three split up and William decided to return to the bivouacked area while Jimmy and Paddy sought out a friendlier bar somewhere at the other end of town.

His hand shook for a moment as he holstered his weapon then parted from his two companions. He wasn't afraid to die, and had proved himself many times in battle yet now for Lydia's sake he must survive. Her letters had shown her fear.

Surely the war would be over soon. William didn't agree with the army's scorched earth policy but it was working and because of it the Boers were weakening and couldn't hold out much longer. He loved Lydia deeply and although her father was rich and threatened to cut her off without a penny, William didn't care. She wrote to him secretly and he knew she felt the same, yet he also knew Lydia would not marry against her father's wishes. Thunder rumbled over the western sky and the rain again splashed on the cobbles.

An alleyway, just past the tavern, led from the main street, a dead end, dark and cluttered with rubbish. The sound of a wooden crate being moved alerted William to the two drunken miners as they sprung from their hiding place. William heard one complain, disappointed that there was just the one British soldier, as he drew his weapon. The first man lunged forward, his knife cutting away part of William's sleeve as he fired back. The man slumped forward, his blood splattering William's uniform. His revolver fell to the ground. The second man rushed.

Using the shot miner as cover William lowered him to the ground and at the same time reached for the miner's knife which was still clutched in his hand. William wrenched the knife free with his left hand.

The second man swore then stabbed wildly at William's right side. The tip of the blade glanced off William's slung rifle butt and threw the man off balance. William twisted and countered with a thrust of the miner's blade. It was a large knife and tore effortlessly into the second man's clothing. William felt the blade slide off ribs and finally lodge itself in the man's chest. The miner gasped and fell without another sound. Both men were dead and as a grim fulfillment of an earlier premonition their blood mingled with the rain that now came down with renewed vigor.

Shaken, William looked around, he doubted anyone would come out of the tavern to investigate, or for that matter had even heard the gun shot fired so close to the miner's body, muffling the sound.

Quickly William searched their pockets looking for plunder. He kept the knife and wiped its blade across the woolen jacket of the second man. He felt the inside pockets which betrayed nothing of importance, no coins, no watch, just a grubby handkerchief that he pulled out and tossed to the ground. The shot miner lay now on his stomach so William felt the pants pockets first and found a few coins. He rolled the man over and after searching the coat's outside pockets felt along the inside of the garment. A few more coins, and a small one shot pistol which William tucked into his own pants pocket. In searching the man's shirt pocket William's hand glanced against something hard on the man's chest; a pouch, hung by a leather thong around the man's neck. William cut the thong away and stuffed the pouch into his own jacket pocket.

He could hear voices coming along the main street, English voices. William hurried. He rolled the shot man back onto his stomach then as a second thought he checked the neck of the second man. He smiled for there too was a leather thong. He cut the thong and pulled a second small bag out from under the blood soaked shirt.

"William is that you?" called Jimmy from the street.

"Aye, those two miners jumped me, tried their best to kill me."

He looked at the two bodies, dark and lifeless. This was a terrible place to die. He holstered his weapon a bit shaken then rejoined his comrades.

"Anything on them?"

"These," said William. And he handed the coins for Jimmy and Paddy to share.

It wasn't 'till later that night, closer to morning actually that he looked at the contents of the pouches. His heart leapt when he saw them; some crudely cut already, others just as they had been dug from the ground; diamonds. Even in the dark he could see their sparkle as the fire light caught their cut faces. He wondered about the miners and decided that if the gems were hidden then they must also have been stolen. A fortune alone in one bag, but with two, William couldn't imagine the wealth. Like their two predecessors William tied them securely around his neck, later he would sew them into his clothing so as to lessen the bulk at his chest.

William picked up his pen. How could he tell Lydia about today? He decided he couldn't, not in a letter anyone might read, so instead he wrote…

* * *

*Fortune has smiled upon us my love. Upon my return I shall confront your father and ask for your hand. He will not deny me. The Boer Guerrillas have taken a beating this day and we are hopeful the war will soon be over. With God's help I will return to you. I think of you every day. Your picture is close to my heart and the sight of you gives me strength.*

*I do so miss you,*
*William*

# Chapter 10

Kate looked at the letter in wonder. The Boer War. Her history knowledge was lacking somewhat in that area but she remembered the unpopular war had started close to the turn of the century. And now here was an actual letter from someone who had lived through it, or at least she hoped he had lived. "Do you think this is Connor's Grandfather?"

Birdie took the letter and stared at the signature. "You mean *my* Great, Great, Grandfather?" He paused for a moment. His eyes suddenly glossed over and he blinked away the forming tears. "Yes, I do."

Kate smiled at him tenderly realizing that at this moment Birdie felt the journey was for himself now and not for Alex Cheyne or his Grandmother. A journey, that would tell him who he was and where he came from…his family.

"Shall we read another?"

Birdie looked at her warmly, "Perhaps another old one."

Kate fingered through the envelope corners again looking for a picture of Edward VII. Between two letters was a single thickness card, a post card. The front had a valiant picture of the brave British soldier. Wounded and alone, surrounded by fierce enemy soldiers, he bravely defended the British flag in his care. It was addressed to Lieutenant William Cheyne, The Cameronian Rifles, South Africa. On the reverse was a lengthy letter written in tiny script to maximize the writing area.

It was difficult to read as some of the print had faded considerably and there were many smudge prints around the edges.

*My Dearest William,*

*I found this postcard in one of the Portobello shops, the one next to the tailors on High street. It felt very patriotic so I chose it for you. I pray you are safe and well as this card greets you from so far away. I long to see you again and feel the warmth of your touch. The days are long without you and I find myself in a constant daze not able to live in the world around me without you. I think of you as we first met at Sir Richard's Ball. You were so tall and handsome in your uniform. I do believe I fell in love with you at that moment.*

*I pray for you each night that God keep you from harm.*

*Father wishes to send me away to visit Aunt Charlotte in Paris. He wants me to forget about you.*

*It will make little difference as to where I am as I will always have you in my heart.*

*Until you return I remain yours,*

*Lydia*

"I wonder who Lydia was?" reflected Kate.

"I'm saddened to say, I don't know."

"I hope they get to stay together, but we've seen what happens when a father objects to a romance that isn't advantageous." Kate noticed that Birdie was nodding off. It had been a long day. She got up quietly leaving him on the deck. After pulling out and readying the sofa bed, Kate gently shook Birdie's arm. He looked so peaceful and child like. She was glad they had talked.

"I'm sorry… I must have just rested my eyes for a moment."

"That's alright. Your bed is ready and we have to get up early tomorrow."

Birdie's overnight bag was sitting on the end of his bed and he smiled his thanks as Kate got him an extra pillow. "Good night," he said, putting his arms around her. Kate reached up and put her arms around his neck and kissed him on the cheek. He smiled, knowing now that all was forgiven and pulled her closer. His lips brushed against her cheek. Kate closed her eyes and felt him caress her other cheek. His lips brushed past her lips teasingly then joined hers in a soft passionate kiss. Kate felt herself sway, her legs weakening. Birdie's arms held her tighter, she could feel his desire rising against her body.

She smiled warmly looking up at him from his embrace her arms still around his neck. His dark eyes were warm and inviting. From habit she felt the fourth finger of her left hand behind Birdie's neck. Her engagement ring was gone now; she had given it to Evan's mother the day of the funeral. She caressed the place it had been for four months. She wanted love again. To be loved and feel love, but she couldn't…not yet. Her eyes met his. "You better get some rest." Then she smiled weakly and left him as his eyes watched her go to her room.

Kate sat on her bed. She felt flushed and cold at the same time. Opening her suitcase, she stared at the door jam that Birdie had slipped into her bag. Then the tears started to come and she couldn't stop them.

It was early when Kate woke to the ringing of her watch alarm. Birdie had slept soundly stirring only once when he thought he heard sobbing then, dismissed it as coming from the apartment next door, probably the television. He had found the pull out bed comfortable enough and was still asleep at seven when Kate put on the kettle. Kate let Birdie sleep a little longer while she got ready for the day's trip to

27 Mason Street. The lodge served meals for the apartment guests which had saved Kate a lot of time in preparing for their trip. Not having to worry about linens and groceries was a luxury you paid for at many northern lodges but today she was glad the service was offered.

She could hear Birdie stirring as she finished up the touches to her makeup at the vanity mirror. “Tea’s made.”

“I could sleep here forever,” came, a groaned reply.

“Hurry up and get ready.” Kate glanced into the living area. “It’s almost breakfast time.” She laughed as the thought of food took hold. “I’ll wait for you down stairs.”

It didn’t take long for Birdie to get ready. Kate had chosen the only window-facing table left in the dining room and now sat admiring the view as Birdie joined her. The parking lot was to the far left then the gravel walkway meandered from there to the lodge office then curved down to the docking area. Many boaters had started out already and most of the breakfast diners were quickly finishing up in anticipation of a day out on the lake.

“What looks good?” Birdie was referring to the menu Kate held in her hand then noticed the cruet of maple syrup sitting next to the other condiments on the table.

“Ah, I know what I’m having.” he said delighted.

Kate smiled as Birdie ordered a large plate of pancakes and sausage. The lake was a teal green and most of the boats that had been securely tied up for the night had already left the docking area. Birdie’s order arrived first and Kate encouraged him to begin and not to wait for her breakfast to arrive. It would be a warm day, the lake was smooth with hardly a wisp of breeze.

There was a continuous flow of traffic towards the end of the lodge’s long lane way as it was shared with a trading post nearby that offered, besides the usual tourist items, ice cream and hot dogs. Kate watched as vehicles negotiated the sharp turn from the main road. She was glad their car was parked further away, closer to the docks. It was then that Kate noticed him. He was driving a different truck, a blue pickup, but it was the same man they had left stranded back at the service centre. He was just reaching the rear of his parked vehicle and heading towards the trading post when Birdie, wondering who Kate was watching, followed her gaze as the man went inside.

“That’s him!” Kate looked at Birdie in disbelief, “How did he find us?”

Birdie didn't wait to finish his meal, "I have to get rid of the car before he sees us. He must have put a tracking device somewhere."

They had to leave before the man came back out. "Why don't you get the car while I check at the desk and see if there's another car rental place nearby."

It didn't take Kate long. They would have to back track a little to North Bay but there was a car rental place there where Birdie could exchange his car for another. Kate wrote down the phone number intending to call and reserve a vehicle while they drove. Once out of the angled lane way they turned east back on the main road towards North Bay. Whether or not they were seen by the thief Kate couldn't tell but if their car was bugged then he would be confident in following his tracking device and not be too concerned if they left the lodge. It was a fifteen minute drive to the car rental store and after a few minutes deliberation Birdie emerged from the building with the keys to a black Ford Explorer in hand. "Ever since I saw his up close I wanted to try one," was his reasoning behind choosing the S.U.V. Now if the car had been bugged anyone who followed would lose the trail in North Bay.

Now was a good time for Kate to admit her suspicion. She was silent for a moment, not knowing how to begin, "Are you sure that was Geoffrey who called you yesterday?"

Birdie had finished adjusting the mirrors and was just doing up his seat belt. "Let me check again." Birdie pressed the incoming call list and as he had said, the last call had been from Geoffrey's cell phone. "Why, is there something wrong?"

Kate wasn't sure if she should share her thoughts about yesterday's call, but if she was wrong, there was no harm done. "Yesterday, when I answered the phone I could hear voices in the background. Someone was asking the caller if he knew what time the Go-Train arrived. When I said 'Hello' again the caller hung up. Birdie looked at her wondering what she meant.

Kate summed up her suspicions. "I think Geoffrey's here, not in Vancouver. I don't think they have Go-Trains there." Kate could see Birdie thinking.

"It's a good thing we changed vehicles then, but if it's true we should expect another call from Geoffrey as soon as our friend loses our trail."

"What about our things at the lodge?" Kate had booked for the lodge's minimum two night stay and now with their new vehicle it wouldn't be wise to be seen at the lodge.

"We have the advantage," smiled Birdie. We

know where he is now, and what he's driving and we know he will probably have followed us to North Bay. Once there he may find out that we switched vehicles but he won't know where we've gone."

"And he didn't see us at the lodge," added Kate, "so he won't know if we go back or not."

"He may watch for us after he realizes he's been tricked and if he asks the owner he'll find out we planned to stay longer, so we better be careful going back."

Before starting out Kate placed the package with all its contents on the back seat. Back at the lodge she had used a white garbage bag that had been under the kitchen sink as a spare, to carry the contents without dropping them. Glad now that she had had the forethought to bring the items downstairs with her Kate was content now to focus on their journey to 27 Mason Street.

It took less than half an hour. After following the directions she had received from the waitress they now drove down Mason Street. Kate felt a little nervous as to how they would be perceived but actually having the items with her she could speak more confidently about her mission to find a descendant of Connor Cheyne.

The driveway at 27 Mason Street was small. It wound around the house down the side to the wooden garage at the back. Two concrete paths separated by a centre area of grass supplied the surface for parking vehicles. Birdie parked their rental near the front entrance. It was just after nine o'clock and Kate hoped they hadn't arrived too early.

She sat in the S.U.V. for a moment after Birdie got out and wondered whether or not to take the package in right away. Before she had a chance to get out, the screen door of the house opened and a woman came out to greet them. Her smile was warm and inviting. She was a small woman, her angular features made more prominent by her petite size. Her hair was graying but Kate could tell in her younger day her hair would have been raven black.

She stepped down the porch steps and greeted Birdie as he came around their vehicle. Kate decided to take the package with her and returned the smile as the woman offered her hand. "It's nice to meet you. I was very curious about the woman who would travel so far to deliver a package." Kate introduced Birdie as her good friend then together they made their way to the front porch.

Yvonne spoke with a heavy French accent. Kate knew there were large French speaking communities in northern Ontario but didn't realize that Sturgeon Falls was officially a bilingual town as about eighty percent of the population was

Francophone, until they had passed the highway signs proclaiming Sturgeon Falls' uniqueness.

It was a warm day so the three sat on the white, wicker, porch chairs. Kate laid the package on the glass cover of the matching oval wicker table. Yvonne had prepared a tray of cookies and some coffee in anticipation of their arrival. As she brought these from the front hall Birdie and Kate arranged the package's contents out so that Yvonne could see them better. Kate took off the gold ring and laid it next to the fabric medals bag.

Yvonne lived in an older home probably built in the '30s or '40s. It had the dated plaster-walled porch with wide arched windows at each end and each side of the short staircase. The flooring consisted of gray painted narrow planks that seemed to be original. The house itself was a small bungalow style with pebble-dashed exterior. It reminded her of her Grandmother's house in the older part of town often referred to as wartime housing.

Yvonne sat between them after pouring out three mugs of coffee then, inviting them to help themselves to cream and sugar set the cookie plate on the table beside the package and its contents. "This looks interesting." She gazed at the contents before deciding to look at the gold ring. "I remember a ring like this," she said. "It was one of the few things of any value my Aunt left her son." She looked at the ring thoughtfully then held it out so that the morning light caught the edge of the inside gold just so. She lowered her granny glasses that had been resting on her head and looked at the ring again more closely. "Only Will's had a different inscription, something about his mother."

Birdie shot Kate a look of disbelief then looked down at his own ring. Hoping her voice sounded calm Kate asked, "What does this one say?" Kate had looked at the ring several times back at the lodge. The shank had shown nothing out of the ordinary, usual hallmark and gold content, but she had not thought to look further. Obviously Birdie had come to the same conclusion and was nervously fingering the ring on his right hand. Kate could tell he was dying to check the inside of his ring for a similar engraving.

"It looks like… 'The cat…' I need to get my magnifying glass," she said and passing the ring to Kate, she went inside.

Kate looked at the ring and this time checked where Yvonne had been concentrating. Under the boss along the circular enclosure she could see some writing and like Yvonne she would also need a magnifier as the print was very small. Moments later she returned with a rectangular magnifying glass and seeing Kate was also interested in the inscription she handed the magnifier to her.

Kate smiled her thanks and then tilted the ring to catch the light. Kate hesitated as she slowly read the line, careful to get it right. "The cats show the way." She said softly. She looked at Birdie, his face was expressionless.

Yvonne Lyonne smiled. "Well that's certainly different. I wonder what it means?"

"And William's ring said something about his mother?" asked Birdie.

"Yes, but I don't remember any more than that." She offered Kate a cookie then added, "That was the only thing he took when he left. I was older than Will by a couple of years and I do remember that day clearly."

"He had argued with his Uncle. He was tired of living here, tired of the boredom. Some of his buddies were using drugs and there were a few that were always getting into trouble but not Will, he and Frank were good kids. They had been friends since they were little. Frank stayed almost another year then he too left." Her face saddened a little, "I never saw him again." She offered Birdie another cookie then looked thoughtfully at the stack of photos. She carefully separated the old pictures stopping at the one showing Connor in his uniform. "So this is my

Uncle Connor." she said warmly.

"Only his name was not Lyonne," added Kate, "It was Cheyne."

"I never knew that," she said, "I often wondered why my Aunt kept her own name. It seemed rather radical for the times. I know they were married because my Grandparents were upset she didn't wait to get married in Canada." Kate looked at Birdie. So they were married in England after all.

"She was my only Aunt and she died so young, a burst appendix." she explained. When my Grandparents died her personal things were brought here, no one else seemed to want them."

Kate was excited now and tried to sound calm, "Do you still have her belongings?"

"But yes, I didn't have the heart to throw her things away. My father was very fond of his sister so boxes of her papers were stored in the attic. I remember seeing them after Will left." She paused as if remembering the moment. "It seems like yesterday."

Birdie, who had been observing most of the visit, now spoke up, "Would it be possible for us to look at her things? It might help us understand..." Birdie chose his words carefully not wanting to reveal that he and Kate had read some of the letters and had been already looking into the family history, "more about the inheritance."

"We need to find Will before September fourteenth." Then Kate added, "Birdie has been sent here by a relative in Scotland to try to locate the missing heir," which wasn't totally untrue.

"Anything I can do to help, I will. The boxes are in the attic, but you're welcome to look through them." Yvonne turned her attention back to the contents of the package, "I'm sure Will would want his Father's things too." Then as if she had forgotten something important she added, "I forgot to mention, Frank's mother said he won't be here until tomorrow."

Kate saw the look of disappointment on her face then suggested, "Maybe we can speak with him tomorrow. We are staying at a lodge nearby so it won't be a problem to come back."

"I'll speak to Frank's mother tonight," she offered. "Why don't you take Anne Marie's things with you along with these, I'm sure Will, will want them now."

It took the better part of an hour for Birdie to climb up into the cramped attic and search for the boxes Yvonne described. There were two, hidden beneath boxes of old clothing, both well labeled as belonging to Anne Marie. Kate stayed at the foot of the attic ladder, steadying it and waited as Birdie lowered the first box to her. It was the size of a shoe box and fairly light in weight. The second box was almost three times the size and considerably heavier. Kate struggled not to drop it as Birdie backed down the wobbly steps guiding the box as Kate secured the bottom. Particles of dust floated around her as a slight breeze wafted down from the open attic door. It didn't seem anyone had moved the boxes for a very long time. With the ladder folded up to its place in the ceiling, Yvonne led the way back outside to the porch area.

"I'm sorry I can't be of more help," she said, "but, maybe you will find out more after looking through these." She handed Kate the smaller of the two boxes. "If you find Will, tell him I would like to see him again, it's been so long."

Before leaving, Kate wrote out her cell number and asked Yvonne to confirm a time to see Frank tomorrow. Kate gave her a warm hug good-bye as Birdie loaded the boxes into the back of the Explorer. Anne Marie's boxes.

# Chapter 11

Once back on the road Birdie confessed his eagerness to check the inside of his ring. "Then again, perhaps his mother had something inscribed in the ring for him before she died." he pondered.

"Then why does this ring…" She had slipped the gold ring back onto her middle finger, "have a different inscription?"

"I don't know." They were approaching the last mile before the lodge could be seen from the highway. "What shall we do, stay one more night or try to find another place to stay?"

There was no telling if the thief had already inquired about them or if he was parked nearby waiting.

The Toreador song from Carmen played its familiar tune. "Geoffrey," he said. Birdie pulled over to the side of the road. "I wondered when you would finally check up on me." He laughed at Geoffrey's reply. "Quite well actually. There's a relative in North Bay, possibly a son, William Cheyne." Birdie's eyes never left Kate as he spoke the convincing lie. "She's been quite helpful. I wouldn't have had this clue without her. No, we have to wait, he won't be home until tomorrow." Birdie smiled, "I think a B&B would be nice too," then he laughed at something Geoffrey said, "I'll let you know if we find anything. Right. Cheer'o"

Birdie placed the phone back on the console and gave a sigh, "You're right, Geoffrey's here."

"What convinced you?"

"Nothing he said really, more in the way he was talking and asking questions, and for a moment I felt he knew we were together before I told him." Birdie started up the Explorer and prepared to continue on to the lodge. "I think our thief has called Geoffrey already and is now in North Bay waiting for instructions, he'll have told Geoffrey what we did to his vehicle and right now Geoffrey is wondering if I was telling the truth."

"Just to be on the safe side why don't we drive through the parking area and see if the blue truck is there. He'll be looking for two of us so take these." Kate handed Birdie her aviator sun glasses and then undoing her seat belt, lowered herself to the floor in front of her seat.

After two passes Birdie stopped in front of the lodge office area and let Kate out with the smaller package then parked further down the parking lot near the docks. No blue truck. Birdie caught up with her just as she was climbing the stairs to their second floor apartment.

"Everything is all taken care of," she whispered as she reached into her pocket for the key to their room. Birdie gave her a puzzled look but waited until they were inside before asking.

"The girl at the desk was very obliging," explained Kate. "I told her that my ex-boyfriend was following me and that he could get pretty violent." She smiled at her cleverness. "I explained that he knew I was coming to this area and I asked her to tell anyone inquiring about me that we left this morning." Kate laughed as she locked their door behind them, "I tried not to laugh when she told me she understood completely because she had an ex just like that."

"Very clever, remind me never to get on your wrong side."

Birdie set the larger box on the kitchenette table then went immediately to the vanity area and turned on the light. The ring forgotten for the past two hours, was now being scrutinized by Birdie who was intent on checking his ring for an inscription. "What do you make of this?" he asked squinting.

Kate joined him at the sink area. "The light is better on the deck." Then excited she said, "Wait! I have a small magnifier attachment on my tweezers." Kate went to her room and returned triumphant holding a small one inch circular magnifier attached to a long pointed pair of tweezers.

Kate handed Birdie the magnifier as together they found a spot on the deck by the screen where the near noon sun was shining through.

Birdie examined the ring. The magnifier helped. His voice was low and as he spoke slow and deliberately, Kate's skin shivered. "Your fate hides within."

Kate repeated the phrase. "What does that mean?"

Birdie looked at her questioningly. "What does yours say again?"

Kate remembered the inscription without removing the ring. "The cats show the way."

"Well, there's a cat on each ring," said Birdie. "I wonder if 'cats' means all three rings somehow?"

"Maybe there are more than three," offered Kate. "And who made the rings?" her voice trailed off.

"Maybe we'll never know.," Then he brightened. "Do you have the family tree chart handy?"

Dutifully Kate went to the other room and brought her chart out to the deck, pen in hand.

"Okay, we know I got my ring from my mother." Birdie circled his mother's name as a source for one ring. Now, Will, got his ring from his mother." He circled Anne Marie's name. "And the one you're wearing was sent by Jean, Connor's mother." He circled Jean's name slowly, wondering what the connection was, if any. "So if we go by the eldest mother, the rings read in order-'The cats show the way'... 'Your fate hides within'... and one about 'a mother'." Birdie shrugged his shoulders and gave Kate a forlorn look.

It was approaching noon and Kate's grumbling stomach reminded her that other than a cookie she had missed her breakfast. "Why don't we break for lunch. We can take the small box with us and check out the contents while we wait."

"You always know the right thing to say." He took Kate into his arms and gave her a warm hug and a soft kiss. "I'm so glad we're here together."

Kate sat across from Birdie, Anne Marie's box sitting between them on the rectangular table, as they waited for their lunch orders. They chose a booth against the back wall of the restaurant but from Birdie's vantage point he could still keep an eye as to who entered and left through the main front door.

Kate looked at Birdie expectantly, "Do you want to open it?"

There was a solemn moment as Birdie stared at the box. He hadn't expected the emotion he felt from this moment. A part of his family was in that box. He motioned Kate to begin.

She untied the string that held the shoe box lid in place then slowly removed the box's covering. It held mostly papers and at the bottom some pictures loose and unframed. "This feels familiar," said Kate, thinking back to her first glimpse of the package's contents. The papers were folded neatly upon each other and showed only a slight yellowing from age.

Kate picked up the first paper. It was a long document and she was careful as she opened it. "A marriage certificate!" Kate smiled at her discovery. As they had surmised by Yvonne's comments the couple had indeed been married in England. Connor Cheyne and Anne Marie Lyonne had been married February 8th 1945 in Exeter, Devon, England. Their addresses were listed as were their father's names and occupation.

Kate handed the certificate to Birdie who looked thoughtfully at the document with a genealogist's eye. Connor's father was Michael, James, Alexander Cheyne-of own means, and Anne Marie's father was Henri Lyonne-fur trapper. "This will mean so much to my Grandmother," he said.

Kate picked up the next paper. "This is interesting. It's a letter from their lawyer confirming Connor's name change." Kate scanned the paper then summarized her findings, "Connor Michael Cheyne became Connor Michael Lyonne September 12, 1945, Niagara Falls, Ontario, Canada."

Kate's quiche arrived first and she pushed the box to Birdie's side of the table to make room as the waitress placed the dish before her. Kate watched fondly as Birdie reached down for the pictures before looking any further at the papers. There was one of the happy bride and groom; Connor in his uniform and Anne Marie in a long elegant white dress with a matching white hat, its small veil drawn back. He sat in a tall-back chair as his wife stood by his side. "They look very happy." he said softly, and he smiled.

The second picture appeared to be from an earlier time. It too seemed to be a picture of a happy couple. In a similar pose the man was in a suit standing behind his wife as she sat regally wearing a fur piece clasped over her left shoulder and a wide brimmed hat that matched her dark jacket and long skirt. It was the same woman whose picture they had found in the package. "I wonder if this is William and Lydia?"

"Maybe it's Anne Marie's parents," suggested Kate.

"No, the photographer's stamp says Edinburgh."

He looked at the third picture in the stack; a

young girl with long black hair crouching over a shot deer, a knife in her hand. Her hair was braided and she had a couple of pheasant feathers tied into the braid on the right side. Beside her was an older man probably her father, dressed in a plaid shirt and jeans, with a buckskin vest. He held a rifle at his side as the two posed over their kill. He handed the picture for Kate to look at.

"Maybe this is another reason Connor's father disapproved of the marriage, she does look rather primitive in this picture. It would be interesting to find her father's marriage certificate and see if he was married to an Indian woman." Kate handed the picture back. "She was beautiful though, I bet all her patients fell in love with her."

There was one last document in the box that Birdie now carefully opened. It was an official military document, Connor Cheyne's discharge paper. There was a medical letter attached to it. Kate nibbled at her quiche her eyes on Birdie waiting for him to finish reading the document.

"This is remarkable! It explains everything."

Kate swallowed then stared wide eyed at Birdie waiting for an explanation.

"Captain Cheyne had been injured, a bullet wound to the head. He seems to have been promoted." said Birdie smiling then continued, "He had recovered from the physical wound but had developed progressive amnesia and at times didn't know who he was. He was discharged January 15, 1945. The army obviously knew who he was but he himself must have finally had no recollection of his family in Scotland."

"It probably wasn't too difficult for him to come to Canada then and leave his family behind. I wonder if he ever remembered his mother?"

"He must have had the odd memory or else why would he write to her."

"Maybe Anne Marie encouraged the contact with family."

"I doubt that," said Birdie, "more likely she encouraged his name change and the break. I'm sure she must have known how his father felt about their marriage."

Birdie's lunch arrived next and for a moment they both were silent reflecting upon the lives they had just found. For the first time since Kate had met him, Birdie didn't seem to care about his food and sat quietly. She smiled softly and reached across taking his hands in hers. "What are you thinking about?"

"I just wish now I had made the effort to research my Grandmother's side of the family more. It would have meant so much more to her while her memory was still in tact…and now it's too late." he answered quietly.

"I'm sure she will appreciate everything we find now. Besides she obviously didn't speak of her brother often and being the person you are I'm sure you would have tried to find out more for her if you'd known." Birdie gave her hand a light squeeze back then, smiled softly at her. His eyes saddened a moment ago now looked at her fondly.

"You're right. Well let's enjoy our dinner. Just think, last week I was in England and now I'm in a beautiful country with a beautiful woman and we have the rest of the day to do as we please." He reached for the maple syrup he had asked the waitress to bring while ordering his meal and gave the French toast and sausage a liberal soaking.

Her lunch finished first Kaye decided to check into renting a boat for the afternoon. The lodge had fifteen-foot aluminum boats for a weekly or daily rental. Each came with a twenty-five horse powered motor and included life jackets and other safety equipment.

The girl at the desk smiled conspiratorially as Kate signed the bill for the rental. She was a pale thin person, almost frail looking. When she spoke there was a hint of an Irish accent in a few of her words and Kate surmised that she probably was from Irish decent. "There was a fellow in here this morning asking for you," she said in a half whisper. "A grizzled sort of guy, mean looking. I told him you had been here but had checked out just before he showed up." She smiled at Kate enjoying the intrigue. She cast a look Birdie's way then offered her opinion, "He's much nicer."

"I think so too," said Kate. Then she noticed Birdie was talking to someone on the phone.

* * *

It was sunny and uncommonly warm for a Scottish evening. Alexander Cheyne sat by the garden pool resting after a tedious golf game. He had wagered several hundred pounds on the outcome and now sat wondering how he could have lost to such a poor player as Charlie Sommerton.

The phone rang and Alex used the outdoor extension. "It's been a while. I was wondering when you would call again."

"We're close to finding Connor's son," came a confident reply. "We'll know by tomorrow where to find him."

So there was an heir. Alex had hoped that the letter from Jean was just an old woman's fantasy. For a moment he was concerned, but then only he and his detectives knew about the contents of her letter. To the rest of the world Alexander Cheyne was the rightful heir to the estate, and if the solicitors hadn't bothered to look for another he certainly wasn't about to help them. Alex was glad to hear that everything was going smoothly. "You'll make sure then he won't be found?" He smiled to himself. Money well spent he thought.

Encouraged now that everything would turn out as planned Alex concluded the conversation, "If you can wrap this up before the end of August I'll add an extra ten thousand." With that he hung up and then waved a greeting to the doctor as he approached Alex from the sitting room doors.

Duncan Cheyne had suffered another stroke late last night and was now bedridden. Soon Alex wouldn't have to worry about hiding his debts from his father. In less than a month he wouldn't have to worry about anything.

* * *

Birdie was just finishing his phone conversation as Kate rejoined him at their booth. "I'll call you again tomorrow." Was all she heard as she sat down. He gave Kate a small sigh as if to indicate he had done his duty. "My sister," he explained, "she goes in for her eye surgery tomorrow. I promised I'd keep in touch while I was here."

Kate felt a flutter of doubt in her stomach. Something wasn't right but she couldn't put her finger on it...just a feeling. In her mind she could see the heroine, trusting and naive being taken down the wrong path. Birdie had confessed his deception but had he told her everything? After all he had been good at deceiving her. He had said earlier that he was calling his sister from her home then told her he had called Geoffrey. Was he telling the truth now or was he still working with Geoffrey?

If only she could check his phone and see if the call had been an incoming call or whether he had called out. She'd check the call history and see what number was dialed. She stared at the phone as Birdie placed it back in his jacket pocket then felt ashamed for doubting him.

"I hope she's okay." Kate managed to ask. Trying to forget her suspicion, she added, "We have a boat for the day. Are you up for an adventure?"

Birdie's face brightened as he swallowed the last of his tea. "Most certainly, but we should probably check the other box before we go, there may be something in it that might be useful for tomorrow."

Kate emerged from her bedroom ready for a boating excursion. Luckily she had packed her small suitcase with lodge activities in mind just in case. She smiled when she saw Birdie in his surfer style swim trunks, mirrored sunglasses and Tilley hat. "I bought these at the hotel gift shop before we left," he explained proudly, "and, I am prepared for all eventualities." With this he fanned his arm out over his suitcase which displayed a variety of drug store items. Sun screen, sun tan lotion, Aloe-Vera gel for sunburn, antibacteria spray for cuts, a small box of bandages, bug repellent and an antiseptic stick for insect bites.

Kate sat down on Birdie's bed next to the suitcase. "Well let's hope we have an occasion to use them." laughed Kate.

Birdie took her hands and pulled her up. He nuzzled her neck as he gave her a tight hug. "You smell delicious." He leaned back and gave Kate a studying look then closed his eyes. "Smells like Amaretto."

"Very good, almond lotion actually." She leaned in returning Birdie's hug which prompted a passionate kiss, then a second that lasted twice as long.

Anne Marie's box had remained on the kitchenette table since they had arrived back from Sturgeon Falls and now the two of them sat at the table hesitant to open it. There was a reverent pause before Kate untied the twine that held its secrets and once unbound she pushed the box toward Birdie who sat at the opposite side of the table.

Kate could see now why the box had been heavier than the first. There were only two items that sat one on top of the other. A rather large wooden box and a leather covered book. Kate waited as Birdie opened the book's cover and read the contents of the first page. " 'This is the journal of William Cheyne, written as a reminder of my blessings, January 1, 1899.' " Birdie fingered the pages as he checked the date of the last entry. The book was almost two inches thick and appeared to cover the years between 1899 and 1939. He looked up from the worn manuscript and gave Kate a blank look. "It belonged to William Cheyne. It's his journal."

Kate smiled; glad now that they had come on this journey and glad now that Birdie had found a part of his family so far from home. "What about the box?"

Birdie sat the book down and turned his attention to the wooden box. It was made with thin sheets of birch and fastened with a brass hasp. It was unlocked and opened easily after what must have been years in a dusty attic. Inside he found a tin box, some loose bullets, regimental insignia, a carved bone, and a Glengarry bonnet. Birdie passed the tin box to Kate.

"A chocolate box!" There was a picture of Queen Victoria on the lid. "I've heard of these," she said. "There was one in an auction house I went to once. Queen Victoria sent every one of her soldiers in

South Africa a chocolate box. In each box was her gift of chocolates and in her handwriting across the bottom it said, 'I wish you a Happy New Year, Victoria Reg.' " Kate carefully raised the lid. "Too bad, no chocolates." Inside were post cards, two medals, and a small stack of letters.

"The Cameronians," said Birdie. He was looking at a regimental cap badge. He carefully fingered the bugle horn and thistles that adorned the badge with the Douglas star prominent above it. "The Scottish Rifles." He sat the badge down and gave Kate a saddened smile. He realized the wealth of information that lay before them and for someone who had attempted genealogy with some success it was overwhelming.

"This is remarkable. This is his life, my Great, Great, Grandfather's life. Look at the history here!"

"These must have been sent to Connor sometime after he married Anne Marie. Maybe she thought her son would one day want to see them and saved them."

"Maybe, maybe there's also a clue as to what the rings mean." Birdie fingered the two medals, both were silver. One had a picture of Queen Victoria with two clasps attached implying the soldier served in two battles; Paardeberg and Johannesburg. The other bore the likeness of the new King Edward VII and also had clasps attached; South Africa 1901 and South Africa 1902. “I think we should read the journal before we give it up,” he suggested.

# Chapter 12

The sun was warm and facing west Kate could take full advantage of the basking rays for sun tanning. There was little wind and the sounds of the lake intensified as she lay on the wooden chaise enjoying the time alone to think. Boaters who had come in out of the midday heat for lunch were soon off again to enjoy the calmness of the water while they could and the drone of the motors faded as the last of the boats left the dock area. The aluminum boat she had rented for the day sat calmly at the dock bobbing gently as if waiting for them. She had brought her phone outside with the intention of calling Kelly, but not knowing what to say she had put it off twice. Better call now she thought or Kelly might have the police looking for her.

The phone rang four times and Kate dutifully listened to the recorded message. "Hi Kel, thought I would call and tell you I'm up north. Everything is okay; I'm just researching for a book idea. Would you please call Simon for me and let him know. I should be back within a couple of days. Kate." She smiled, thankful that she didn't have to go into a long involved conversation with her sister.

The door to the deck opened and Birdie entered. He looked tired and a bit saddened.

"What they went through. I could never imagine doing some of the things they had to do during the war."

Kate made a place for him on the chaise as she slipped on her robe then sat back with her knees drawn up to make more room. "You mean the Boer War."

"Yes, it's all so sad. Michael still had nightmares about the war. Even ten years later it still affected him. He witnessed Boer farms being destroyed, their animals slaughtered, homes being fired, and the women and children sent to inhumane containment camps."

He spared Kate some of the horrendous details of the journal and chose his words carefully as he told her of a soldier's life in South Africa. The archaic way the generals led the men in battle. Many were veterans of the Crimea War, and to fight the old way in an age where the enemy had modern weapons was suicidal. There were so many needless deaths. The treatment of the Boer woman and children even drew scorn from the British population when it was discovered that they were herded into camps and given nothing, not even fresh water in many cases.

The military policy was a scorched earth policy and if they could gain victory by burning everything and destroying everything then they would do it.

Kate listened as Birdie told her more of the content of the first fifty pages he had read so far. "Michael was almost killed, not in battle but by two miners that were drunk and out to get him. They waited for him outside a bar but luckily he overpowered them. They both died. He says in his journal that he could still see their faces as they were in the alley that night."

Then Birdie smiled at her. "He married his sweetheart Lydia after all and they lived near Edinburgh. Apparently he came into some money after the war and her father allowed their marriage." He reached into his pocket and pulled out a folded piece of paper, yellowed with age. "And I found this.' He held the paper up triumphantly then passed it to Kate. "It fell out from between two pages in the journal."

Carefully Kate opened up the paper to find that it was a receipt. A receipt for three rings made to order by Gilmour and Watson, Mitchell Street, Glasgow, dated 1925. She looked at Birdie then smiled in disbelief, "Three rings!"

"Yes, but I'm afraid this just creates a lot more questions. Why three and for what purpose? Why bother to send them to Connor? What do the inscriptions mean?"

"Maybe there'll be something in the rest of the journal to help with those questions," offered Kate. "In the mean time, let's go for a ride, it's time for a break." Kate smoothed down her robe and prepared to get up taking the journal from Birdie's hands. "Why don't you get changed and I'll see if the kitchen can make us up a snack."

Birdie's tired look had brightened and he gave Kate a big hug before she took the staircase from the deck down to the office area. There was something he had to do first.

"Geoffrey, it's me. Yes, I couldn't talk before. No, she doesn't suspect anything yet, but she is a help. I should have more information about Connor's son tomorrow. When will you be back? I should know by then. Don't call me. Right."

It was almost one-thirty but the kitchen was able to quickly prepare a small picnic lunch for the two. Kate carried the thermal bag down to the boat where Birdie was waiting. He had taken the initiative and asked one of the boat mechanics to instruct him on the use of the small motor and equipped with this knowledge and a small photocopied map he found in the boat house, stood confidently awaiting his passenger.

The motor was idling on low so Kate didn't question the seating arrangements and just accepted Birdie's hand as he helped her onto the flat aluminum seat in front of him. Dressed in his excursion outfit Kate couldn't help smiling. He was so unlike anyone she had met before. She smiled at his eagerness, all her doubt about his motives vanished as she enjoyed the moment. "Would you care to be the navigator?" He offered the map to Kate, who turned around on the seat and faced the front for a better view of the lake.

"That way I think," and she pointed the way. As they left the dock area and passed the man-made gravel island that helped to shelter the docks, there were two small islands on their right that seemed to join at the end of a narrow bay. Past them according to the map was a larger island set back so it wasn't immediately seen from the lodge. They passed a boat with two fishermen and Birdie enthusiastically waved back a greeting.

As they approached the larger island Birdie immediately slowed down having been warned by the mechanic about numerous rocks that lay submerged around the island, and could easily put a hole in their boat or damage the motor's propeller. There was little breeze, which made maneuvering around the island easier until they came to a suitable landing spot. There was a small sandy area on the west side of the island and Birdie guided the small boat between two rocks then shut off the motor as they glided along the strands of wild rice until coming to a stop in a few inches of water.

"Allow me." He said gallantly, then, stepped out jolting Kate as she sat clutching the seat along the edges. He pulled the boat up further onto the sand and then offered his hand to Kate. She passed him the picnic basket first then, taking his hand, followed him onto the warm soft sand. The water was warm and it was near the end of August which meant they would probably not be bothered by mosquitoes or black flies.

Birdie had thought to bring some of his drug store items, a blanket from their room and two large towels in case they decided to swim.

A boater zoomed by and waved a 'Hello'. Their island, unlike the two they had passed was mostly rock with some grassy patches, low shrubs and a few large pine trees. It rose in the centre so that you couldn't see the island as a whole which gave them the feeling of being alone. Crows had taken up roost in the pine tree nearest them and squawked continuously as if protesting their invasion until finally one flew off to the other side of the island and the rest followed.

A seagull knowing that humans often meant

food landed on their beach and with its head nodding started his loud screeching. He cautiously approached Kate and Birdie but found no reward in his efforts. Others, hearing the commotion circled in the air watching, waiting for some scraps. "Don't feed them yet," warned Kate, "or we'll be overwhelmed by more."

Finally seeing no benefit in staying, the seagulls abandoned their attempt and left, all but the first bird who patiently sat waiting in the water, occasionally dipping his head below the surface in search of small fish.

"I'm glad we came out, the reading was making me tired, but I should try to get through the rest before tomorrow just in case there is something important." Kate had stretched out the blanket and now sat next to Birdie. Birdie sat the picnic lunch container between them as they sat just far enough away from the lapping water on the warm sand.

"I found out her name was Lydia Sutherland. Her father was very rich and objected to her marrying beneath her." Birdie started to fish out the contents of the thermal bag and made a contented sound of approval.

"I saw that name on the computer," she said. Kate took the beef sandwich Birdie offered her then helped herself to one of the two drinks that were packed. "I checked the crest motto on the ring I had and it was their name that came up. It's the Sutherland crest."

"That's interesting." Birdie was silent for a moment. He bit into the sandwich lost in thought and stared out to the lake. He had seen the photo on her night table while searching the house for thieves and now Birdie wanted to ask Kate about the young man in the photo. The young man who seemed so full of life and now, he knew, was just a memory. He knew too he couldn't compete with a memory. A memory was perfect and pulled you back into the past. It made resisting the present possible and Birdie wanted to be a part of Kate's present… and her future. He wanted to ask more about the young man in the frame who sat next to her bed each night, but didn't. He could wait…he would have too.

Instead he tossed the remains of his crust to the eagerly awaiting seagull, then smiled at Kate as she laughed at the bird's attempts to recover the scattered tidbits floating on the water.

A musical interlude played and Kate quickly put down her sandwich and searched her cover-up pocket for her phone. "Hello?" There was a pause and Birdie could hear a female voice speaking and surmised it was probably Yvonne Lyonne.

"Tomorrow at ten? That would be fine.

Number 73. Yes, thank you." She tucked her phone back into her pocket and then gave Birdie a big grin. "We meet Frank tomorrow at ten o'clock. His mother lives just up the street from Yvonne, number 73" She smiled at Birdie, "Check out is also at ten, which means we have until tomorrow to enjoy this beautiful place."

"In that case I'm glad I came prepared," and he searched in his bag of supplies until he found the suntan lotion. "I'd like to come here again sometime," he said wistfully. "We have lakes at home of course but nothing like this, these seem different somehow." He smiled, then handed Kate the lotion.

The remainder of the afternoon was spent swimming, exploring smaller islands, and feeding seagulls remaining bits of their lunch. They were becoming friends and for the moment Birdie was content with that. His body wanted more and he thought he could feel her respond in kind with every kiss but dared not rush her.

They got back in time for the supper service. Kate had been proud of Birdie's ability to master the skill of boating so quickly. After supper he planned to fish off the dock for a while after hearing a fisherman at the next table talk about the big one he caught the previous night while his boat was tied up at the dock.

Kate decided to join him down by the boats and sat in one of the lodge's colourful wooden chairs, journal in hand while Birdie fished.

He was using jigs and a rod that the boat mechanic had loaned him and stood now triumphant as he held up his first catch of the evening, a three inch perch. "I've never fished before," he had told Kate and now after a bit of casting practice, looked like a pro.

Kate opened the journal where Birdie had marked the next page to be read.

*Dec 2, 1905,*

*I spoke with my old friend Toshie yesterday. I haven't seen him since the party at Reggie's two years ago. We talked about his work and he was very interested in my design for the table I wanted to make. He had not made this kind of table before and was quite interested by the idea of making one for me. He said it would look a bit different to his usual designs with the brass decorations and extra drawers I had in mind but we will meet tomorrow to discuss my ideas.*

*Dec 3, 1902,*

*Saw Toshie today and he was delighted with my ideas and thought he could design a table that included my need for secrecy. I will see the final drawings within the next few weeks. I am excited that this burden will be hidden and I will rest much easier once the table is made.*

Kate read on and discovered that he had the table made in time for Christmas this year. After turning the third page she flipped through the rest of the book and there stuck between two pages she found the receipt for the table. She carefully unfolded the taped yellowed paper. The receipt was typed and signed by C. Mackintosh.

Kate didn't know a lot about antique furniture but she did know enough from attending auctions with her friend who was interested in mission furniture, that a table made by Charles Rennie Mackintosh could fetch close to a possible million. The receipt described one custom made table with brass cat designs on the legs and surface of the table and a secret compartment built in as per the client's request. A puzzle-table, cost 135 pounds.

Why would William Cheyne want a puzzle table if not to hide something precious to him. William Cheyne had been a lieutenant during the Boer War. How had he gained enough money to eventually buy the Cheyne estate? How had he convinced Lydia's father to permit their marriage? Kate didn't know, but somehow he had come into money.

Kate saw Birdie on the dock casting toward the gravel island in hope of a hit. She was eager to tell Birdie the news about the table but the journal enticed her to read on a little further first. She went back to the place where she had left off. The next ten years showed nothing too eventful other than the birth of his children. William had contacted a few of his war buddies, had bought some land surrounding his estate, had gone to France on business eight times and was still having nightmares about the war in Africa.

Then in mid 1918 Lydia came down with influenza and died survived by her husband and two sons, Michael and Duncan.

The next few pages were written by a man obviously grief stricken. It told of a man empty and lost with growing disdain for his youngest son's wastrel habits. Kate read on, intrigued. Michael had married well but was a weak man easily angered and easily led, while Duncan had taken to drinking and womanizing. He soon married a family friend's daughter whom he had gotten pregnant. In 1922 Michael and Jean had a son Connor, a delight to his Grandfather.

Then she found it, a reference to the rings he had made by a jeweller in 1928.

*Nov 12, 1928*

*I go to Glasgow tomorrow to pay for the rings I had commissioned. I must decide today what the inscriptions are to be. I have taken steps to protect the Cheyne fortune, as sadly, my sons are a disappointment to me but my Grandson Connor remains a hope for the family. It is for him I leave everything that I have. He is such a joy to me.*

"Birdie!" Kate jumped up and ran to the dock slip where Birdie was standing. It was getting dark now but the flood light from the lodge office illuminated the whole of the dock area. She paused, then before joining Birdie on the dock she slipped the table receipt into her pocket. For now she would keep the information found about the puzzle table's receipt to herself; there would be plenty of time to share the table's description after they talked to Frank.

Frank Stone must have been around sixty-five. He was a tall, thin man yet fit and his dark eyes and complexion revealed his native heritage. He gave Birdie and Kate a warm greeting and offered them a seat on his front porch. His mother, an elderly gray haired lady with a significant stoop presented the three with some coffee and cake then left to go back to her laundry.

"Will, always longed for adventure. He was tired of the north. I suppose there were other things he could have done up here but all he saw was the boredom and the lives ruined by drink and drugs." He looked wistfully around at the homes, the distant forest with its rolling hills. "He never saw living here as an adventure."

Frank picked up his coffee mug and seemed to be thinking of the past as he stared into the coffee. "Will had been my friend for as long as I can remember. We grew up together, joined the US Army together, went to Nam together and survived. Will got married and stayed in Toronto after the war; his wife's brother had a job for him. I lost track of Will after that, until he wrote to me here. I got his letter a year or so later as I'd been wandering out in Alberta doing odd jobs, deciding what I wanted to do with my life." He seemed saddened all of a sudden... remembering. "War changes you. Nothing seemed important any more. Will was the lucky one. He met a nice girl and got married. I saw him only twice after that." He reached for the cake dish and offered some to Birdie and Kate, then took another piece for himself, "Once shortly after his son was born and the last time in '92 before he died."

Kate felt a flood of sadness come over her and she saw Birdie had the same sorrowful look.

"He came down with cancer, brain cancer I think and died shortly after it was diagnosed. I blamed it on the war, we didn't know until years later about all the poison the military dumped on us over there."

"Maybe not," said Kate, "Will's Grandfather

Michael, also died of a brain tumor." Then a thought occurred to her, "Does Yvonne realize Will is dead?"

Frank smiled, "Yes, she does but prefers to think of him as one day coming back," then he shrugged, "so I don't challenge her delusion, it's a comfort to her."

Birdie and Kate shared a glance for a moment then Birdie asked, "Do you remember Will's wife's name?" he asked.

"Queenie, her name was but after the funeral she never bothered to keep in touch." then he shook his head, "Maybe that's not fair, maybe she did but I was away." He sat his coffee mug down on the table, "I did try once, but she had moved away from the area. A neighbour told me she had gone to stay for a while with her married sister but I never knew their names. If you find her, tell her I was asking about her and if she would like to get in touch she can call me." Then his face brightened, "Maybe I can relate some stories about Will to his son." This sudden grain of purpose showed as he quickly fetched a pen and scrap of paper from inside the house. He added his mother's phone number as well as his cell number and folding it handed it to Kate who took the paper gladly.

"Yvonne has my number too." With that said Kate and Birdie stood up and thanked Frank for his help and hospitality.

# Chapter 13

"Well, where to?" asked Birdie as they left Frank's driveway.

"I guess back home to St. Catharines. I don't remember seeing a Queenie Lyonne in the list of names I found, but maybe someone will know her. Then again maybe she remarried but without knowing their son's name this might be the end of our search." Kate thought of the few phone calls she had made already and didn't feel comfortable in calling them again, especially the family with the baby.

"Knowing Connor has a Grandson, is that enough to set the lawyers working to name an heir?"

They turned on to the main road now and were heading back toward North Bay, then south to home.

"Maybe, so far all we have is hear-say. There should be records, though; of Will's death, his marriage and even his son's birth, but we're back to where we started, looking for someone in Ontario, at least with Connor we had a name." He pulled into a parking area beside a small store on the corner of the highway. "It will take a lot of inquiry to find out what we need to know and don't forget we're not direct relatives."

"I will contact a solicitor I know in Edinburgh and see if we can get something started before its too late." he assured her.

"Would you like some snacks for the road," suggested Birdie, unbuckling his seat belt prepared to gather a variety of munchies for the trip.

Kate was deep in thought and didn't answer. "Isn't Queenie usually a nickname?"

"For the Queen you mean…Elizabeth?"

Kate sat staring out the front window appearing not to hear him. He smiled at her concentration then went to find some snacks.

The ride home was uneventful; no phone calls from Geoffrey, no strange man tailing them and no excitement at a rest stop they used on the way home. They managed to get a table by a window and together they sat enjoying roasted chicken and fries.

Kate had been fairly quiet during their drive so far and sat focused on a particular French fry that tried to disappear beneath its ketchup blanket. "William's wife would be in her sixties now, so she would have been born before Elizabeth." She stabbed at her prey. "No… not Elizabeth…Victoria!" she exclaimed triumphantly holding up her quarry. "V. Lyonne was a widow too. I'll bet that's her!" She grinned knowing now they had their next destination…Grimsby.

They were just south of Orillia when Birdie suddenly hit the steering wheel with his right hand. Their vehicle swerved closer to the centre line. Startled, Kate looked up from the notepad she had been writing in. "Sorry." He looked upset. "I can't believe what a fool I've been!" His tone suggested something serious had happened.

"It wasn't the car at all. He knew I'd be expecting a call from him after we exchanged vehicles…and he called hoping I'd feel secure in my supposition."

He glanced at Kate, the Explorer steadied in his hands, "It's the phone…no wonder he insisted on getting for me!"

Suddenly Kate realized what he was referring to. "You mean Geoffrey bugged the phone too?" she said half to herself. "We have to get rid of it." Birdie lowered his window then retrieving his cell phone from the console, prepared to toss the instrument out the window.

"Wait!" Her first impulse was the same as Birdie's. Surely now Geoffrey knew they had been to see Frank and Yvonne, but now there was a chance to lead him on a wild goose chase, if they were lucky, besides she wanted to have a look at it first. "We might be able to use this to our advantage. If we throw it away, eventually Geoffrey would know we just ditched it but if we could send the phone off in the wrong direction he would have no reason to think you didn't still have it. Even if he called and you didn't answer he would think that you just couldn't talk at that moment."

Calmer now, Birdie nodded in agreement, "So what do you propose we do?"

There was a gas station coming up on their side of the road. "Pull in here," she said quickly before they had passed it. "Okay, we get some gas and while we're doing that we wait for another car to stop and plant the phone in their car." In theory this sounded simple but the next vehicle that pulled in was another S.U.V. which parked directly behind them and had two passengers besides the driver and would probably be able to see any suspicious moves by Kate. Another car pulled into the gas station this time opposite them. There was a narrow island which housed the row of pumps that separated the two vehicles.

The driver was a young man. He was alone and the windows of his car were rolled down on this warm August afternoon. Birdie handed the phone to Kate then proceeded to fill up their Explorer. Now, she thought and she turned her back to Birdie, smiling at the young man as he flipped open the gas tank cover and inserted the gas nozzle into his car.

Kate pretended she was making a call, as she quickly hit the menu button, found the call history and checked the outgoing calls. Two since their stay at the lodge, one to Birdie's sister in England, she smiled then, saw the one to Geoffrey, yesterday, before they went out on the lake. Why would he be calling Geoffrey when she wasn't around? Quickly she turned off the phone.

She turned back again towards Birdie, still pretending she was talking to someone. Birdie watched the young driver replace the nozzle then head to the small building at the far side of the pumps that housed the gas station attendant. If she kept the pump between her and the S.U.V. behind them, she could keep out of site as she neared the young man's car.

Birdie watched as the attendant greeted the man and prepared the bill. "Now!" he whispered urgently. Kate turned toward the car and adjusted her purse in front of her at the same time as she tossed the phone onto the floor of the back seat area. She searched her purse looking for her credit card as she passed the young man coming out of the building. He smiled at her as he held the door open and she smiled back.

"I can't believe you did that," said Birdie

proudly, as if praising a promising protege.

"Maybe I've found a new career... Pennington, Kate Pennington...Secret Agent." She laughed at the thrill of it all. "Well hopefully Geoffrey will have a fun time following him." Birdie started the car after Kate fastened her seat belt then they were once again on the road south.

"What do you think made Geoffrey double cross you?"

"Money, probably, though why Alex would choose to work with just one of us, I don't know. How he even knew about Geoffrey to begin with...I guess Geoffrey must have contacted him seeing more in it than I had offered to pay him."

"Well, we should be alright now unless Geoffrey was sitting in his car watching us go through this charade," then she laughed thinking the whole thing suddenly very funny.

Her mood changed just as suddenly when she thought back to the phone history she had seen on Birdie's phone, "Why did you call Geoffrey yesterday?"

Birdie glanced at her then refocused on the road. "You checked my phone?" he asked accusingly. Then his voice softened, "I suppose you had a right to." Birdie checked his mirror as he passed a slower car ahead of them then pulled back into the right hand lane. "I wanted him to think I trusted him, that I was using you to get to Connor's son. I was hoping to stall for time and told him not to call me, that, I would keep in touch." He glanced at Kate, his face showing his emotion, "I'm sorry, I should have told you."

"Yes, you should have," she said quietly but the disappointment was there. Kate wasn't actually that upset now she knew the truth but thought it opportune to make Birdie squirm a little…he deserved it. She expected honesty, especially after his confession at the lodge.

"I am sorry," he said again, glancing quickly at her then back on the road.

They drove; each silent for a few minutes until Birdie broke the heavy mood that hung between them. "Are we off to Grimsby then or back to your house?"

Kate was thinking, wondering how much Geoffrey really knew about their search. Had he gone to see Yvonne Lyonne? Did he follow them and speak to Frank Stone? She fingered the ring on her right hand, the small cat smooth against her finger. "Do you think Geoffrey knows about Connor's name change? Would he have the nerve to just show up and talk to Frank?"

"Oh, he has both the nerve and the ability to put two and two together. We just have to get to

Victoria's house before he does." He shook his head slowly, "I don't think he would actually do anything violent to her son but then again money can make people do irrational things, we don't know what deal he made with Alex…I don't want to take the chance."

Three hours later and they were in Hamilton. Once across the Burlington Skyway Kate checked on her phone for the address of V. Lyonne. "We exit at Bartlett Avenue."

It was just after three o'clock and the traffic had been traveling along at a constant if only 50 kilometres at times, at least it wasn't at a stand still. The day was bright and clear and promised to remain that way for the rest of the day. Kate and Birdie hadn't said much during their drive south and Kate could feel the awkwardness between them.

"Left here," she said after driving toward the lake along Bartlett. "The next one, Eighth Street." They pulled into a long narrow lane that looked more like someone's driveway than a street. There were three houses along the street. Victoria Lyonne lived in the third house.

In its day it had been a beautiful two and a half story early twentieth century framed house, but now it showed its age by lack of repair and upkeep. The paint was faded and the grounds lacked a gardener's care. The wide wrap-around porch which hugged the side and front of the house sagged slightly at one end. But the view made up for any deficiencies the house might have had. Sitting on the edge of the property the house overlooked Lake Ontario, the property cut away at a sharp angle caused by the years of lake water erosion. She could see the tops of several willow trees peeking up beyond the grassy yard that someone had planted years ago probably attempting to keep the soil in place.

Birdie chose a spot behind the house that seemed designated for parking. He unbuckled his seat belt then held the steering wheel as if focused on the small dial in the centre. "I don't know what to say...if this is the right person, she would be my mother's cousin." Then he looked at Kate and smiled. "This is suddenly becoming all too real. I mean before we were finding people who were… well…ancestors, but now we're finding people who may become part of my life."

"A little worried are you," Kate took his hand in hers, "that maybe you won't like them?"

"Something like that, I never expected to find anyone, I guess."

"Well let's go and meet them." Kate could see someone at the curtained window, possibly wondering who they were as well.

Their side door appeared to be the most used entrance to the house as it was closest to the parking spot. Kate looked around and wondered if they should walk to the lake side of the house where the formal entrance should be, when the wooden paneled door opened and a young woman looked at them cautiously.

"Please excuse us," started Birdie, "we're looking for a Victoria Lyonne."

"I'm Vicky Lyonne." The young woman seemed in her late twenties. Her dark hair was up and held in place with a wide clip. Her eyes were dark and Kate couldn't help but notice a resemblance between her and Yvonne Lyonne. The younger woman noticed the puzzled look on Birdie's face, "Perhaps it was my mother you were looking for… Victoria."

"Who is it Vicky?" came a voice from a room near by.

"Come in, won't you."

They were led down a narrow hallway that passed by smaller rooms on either side then flowed into a dining area which lay open adjacent to a very large kitchen that spanned the width of the house. Windows wrapped around the perimeter giving the kitchen an outdoorsy spectacular view. The windows were old but the rest of the kitchen looked newly renovated. Victoria Lyonne was busy at the central island preparing a casserole of some kind. She had seen them enter and was wiping her hands on a nearby towel in preparation to greet them. Kate thought Victoria must be in her mid sixties but surprisingly didn't look it. Her skin was clear and her hair, tucked up neatly by combs while she was cooking, was a light brown in colour and showed no trace of gray. Her blue gray eyes showed a vibrancy as she smiled at Kate. Victoria had kept up her appearance and could easily pass for fifty.

"Mother, these people would like to speak to you."

Kate took the initiative, "Hello," she took the hand Victoria offered then quickly introduced herself and Birdie using his Christian name instead. They were motioned to the dining area where there was enough room for them to sit comfortably.

The two women looked at her expectantly. "I'm not really sure where to begin," she started, "if your husband's name was William Lyonne, then I believe …" she nodded at Vicky, "you and Robin are cousins."

Birdie continued, smiling warmly at the two, deciding now that he did like them, "We believe that William was the heir to an estate in Scotland and that his son…" Birdie hesitated, Frank had said Will had

had a son, was he alive? Victoria's eyes were still focused on him and showed no change at the mention of her son so he continued, "by being a direct descendant of Connor Lyonne will now inherit this property."

Vicky's eyes had grown larger after hearing this news while Victoria shook her head in disbelief. "Was it you who called me the other day?" she asked Kate.

"Yes," said Kate, "and we've been searching for you since then." Then thinking to add a bit of weight to their presence she added, "Robin's been sent to search for Connor Lyonne or his son." Kate went on to quickly tell the story of their quest; the package, Connor's name change, his Grandfather's will and the importance of doing something before time runs out.

Victoria smiled almost in disbelief, "I never knew any of this, about William's people, I mean. He never spoke of them, I often wondered why." Then she shook her head wondering, "Then maybe he never knew himself, he was raised by Pierre Lyonne, and they didn't know his father, so I guess there wasn't much to pass on."

She took Vicky's hand in hers and gave it a joyful squeeze, "Michael will be so pleased!" Then as if she had suddenly forgotten something important she rose from the table, "I'm forgetting my manners. Here you've been driving for hours...would you like some tea or coffee?"

Birdie's eyes lit up, "Thank you, yes, tea please."

Tea and biscuits were prepared and the next half hour was spent with Victoria and Vicky sharing stories about Mike Lyonne. He lived in Niagara Falls with his wife and three year old child. Right now he was working in Alberta while his little family stayed with his wife's sister. Wages for qualified pipe fitters were too good to pass up and with Mike gone for three months; he would make enough money to hopefully put a down payment on a new home.

Victoria set down her tea cup then looked thoughtfully at Birdie, "Would it mean Mike would have to go and live in Scotland?"

Truthfully Birdie told her he didn't know the conditions, whether occupation of the estate was mandatory or whether it could be sold, although that possibility seemed a sad option after all the trouble his great, great Grandfather had gone to in order to keep it safely in the family.

"We need to start proceedings as soon as we can," explained Birdie. "You will need to speak to Mike about returning as soon as possible then gather all the documents he will need before flying to

Scotland." Then he grinned widely, "I expect this will be a bit of a shock."

"Yes," said Victoria, then she smiled softly and held her daughters hand, "It's been difficult for all of us since Will died. He was ill for a long time too and it affected all of us."

Then she seemed to focus back on the task presented to her, "I have our marriage certificate and Michael's birth certificate here in the house."

"The only document we don't have is Will's birth certificate, unless it's with some of the papers in Anne Marie's box," offered Kate. "There's a marriage certificate for Connor and Anne Marie and a lawyer's document regarding his change of name."

Then a thought occurred to her, "Does Mike have an up to date passport?"

"I believe he does because he and Danielle often go across the border in Niagara Falls to shop."

"On second thought, this might not all be necessary. I mean Mike might not have to return so soon, or even go to Scotland." said Birdie. "I will call my solicitor and see what is required. Perhaps it can all be taken care of from this end." It was nine in the evening back in Britain and Birdie wouldn't be able to call until first thing in the morning. "I will phone tomorrow morning and get back to you as soon as I find out something."

Kate had noticed Birdie finger the ring on his right hand and knew he was thinking the same thing she was. She held her ring out for Victoria to see it. "Does Mike have a ring like this," she inquired.

Victoria smiled when she saw the cat relief on the surface. "No, I have it upstairs in my jewellery box. Shall I get it?"

"Please, if you don't mind."

"I'll go Mother." Vicky left the table and quickly made her way up the staircase to the next floor.

While she was gone Birdie and Kate explained the cat ring mystery. Victoria had never looked at the ring that closely and had no idea there was any inscription hidden under the boss. Vicky returned, her face beaming with excitement, and placed the ring in her mother's hand.

"Here, you'll probably need these." said Kate as she fumbled in her purse to retrieve her tweezers magnifier. "The writing's small and goes around the edge underneath."

Victoria took the proffered magnifier and went to the dining room window where the light was better. She was silent for a moment while turning the ring in a better position to catch the light. "Your Mother Holds the Key." She read it again slowly then looked at Birdie and Kate, "Is that right? What does it mean?"

"We're not sure," offered Kate. "It was a clue to something, created by..." she smiled, "Robin and Mike's Great, Great, Grandfather, but that was back in the '20s, it may be nothing more now than just a family keepsake"

Victoria looked at the ring thoughtfully as she sat down then handed it to Vicky to look at. "The Cats Show the Way…Your Fate Hides Within…Your Mother Holds the Key." She shook her head slowly, "It does sound interesting, very mysterious."

Birdie smiled warmly at her, "Yes, it does. Then his face took on a serious look. There's something I feel I have to warn you about." He looked at Kate who nodded slightly then resumed, "There is a man following us who would like to keep the status quo regarding the estate." He explained Geoffrey's attempts at getting information while playing down his own involvement in the matter; it would do no good to confuse them of his intent. "Geoffrey may have followed us here and may show up later posing as someone else." He looked into those blue gray eyes that suddenly became anxious, and Birdie reached across and took her hands in his, "There's not much he can do anyway, now that we know the truth, but please be careful."

# Chapter 14

After another hour of enlightening Victoria and Vicky as to their family history, Kate and Birdie took their leave. Kate had left Victoria Frank's phone number after describing his attempt to contact her and hoped she would call him. Vicky was thoroughly delighted that they had found some of her father's family and was eager to visit Cousin Yvonne in Sturgeon Falls. But they could also feel a sense of uneasiness that they had left the mother and daughter. Better for them to know the truth though and be prepared.

"Well, what do you think?" asked Kate, once they were back on the Queen Elizabeth Highway towards St. Catharines. Birdie hadn't stopped grinning since he left their house.

"It's all a little overwhelming. I never expected to find another part of my family." He glanced at Kate before passing a slower vehicle on the right. "They are very nice, and I know this will make a difference in their lives especially Mike's, not just the money I mean, but give them a sense of belonging." He reached out and squeezed Kate's hand.

"It's made a difference in mine too."

"I'm glad, but what do we do now? Should we go to my house or your apartment or stay somewhere else?" She was resisting a look over her shoulder, "Do you think it's safe?"

Kate could see Birdie's mind working as he drove, calculating the odds of Geoffrey waiting for them as they returned to Kate's house. "Can you get into your house through the back door?"

"Yes, I have a key and we can go through the neighbour's yard from the street one over."

"Good, so if we parked a street away and walked to the backyard, we shouldn't be seen. Once inside we'll leave the lights off." He nodded to himself. "We should be all right, unless our friends are waiting quietly on your street for us to come back."

"I know how I can check," suggested Kate, "I'll call Mr. Whitmore and ask him to check the street for us and let us know if there are any strange cars parked there."

"Good plan."

They drove for a few minutes then decided to stop for some food before reaching Kate's house. Just off the exit to Beamsville was a large supermarket where Birdie pulled into the parking area near the main entrance. "I'll wait in the car for Mr. Whitmore's call." offered Birdie. Ten minutes later Kate was back with what smelled like roast chicken. "Mmmm," said Birdie, "can't wait for supper."

He helped Kate reach the back seat with the two bags she carried. "Everything's all right. The street looks clear, but just to be safe we'll go the back way." Kate nodded in agreement. "I'll drop you off and then park a couple of blocks away."

Kate's neighbours were good friends and she had no difficulty cutting across their back yard and using the mutual gate they had installed two years ago, to get to her back deck.

While waiting for Birdie she called her neighbour to let her know about Birdie coming and then Mr. Whitmore to fill him in briefly as to their plans.

Birdie arrived just as Kate was setting out the food she had bought, barbecued chicken, potato salad, green salad, and a baguette. She had closed any door that might show their presence to the front of the house and then positioned a few battery candles around them ready for nightfall. The back deck was closed in and quite warm after the westerly midday sun. It opened up to a smaller room off the kitchen and it was here that Kate set up their supper, the same place they had had their first breakfast. She opened a bottle of white wine and set out two glasses, deciding not to open the refrigerator again and allow unwanted light to filter through the house.

"This looks lovely, and I'm famished."

Together they enjoyed their chicken dinner. There was a small corduroy love seat on the deck and afterwards as they sat enjoying the sunset Kate and Birdie recalled the events of the past two days. "So, now what?" asked Kate.

"We won't know anything until I call Mr. Bean tomorrow and see where things stand legally."

Kate erupted into laughter and almost spilled the wine in the glass she was holding.

"I'm sorry, but you did say Mr. Bean." She said giggling until her eyes watered.

"Oh, I see," then he smiled too at the thought of Rowan Atkinson's character conducting law. "I assure you, my Mr. Bean, Jacob Bean has the highest credentials as well as being a dear friend." Still hunched Kate tried hard to calm her laughing.

"Oh, I needed a good laugh," she sat up clutching her side, "oh, that hurt."

She picked up her wine glass, "How soon can we call him?"

"They're six hours ahead of us, so any time after 4 a.m. should be all right" It was almost nine o'clock now and the last remnants of the red and pink sky were fading into a deep navy. A bright moon could be seen just rising past the roof of the house behind hers. In a few minutes it would cast a warm light into her deck.

Birdie sighed after finishing the last of his wine. "It's been a very long day, I can barely remember this morning."

"You must be tired after all the driving we've done." He looked tired but happy.

"Come here, partner." He raised his left arm up resting it on the rounded back of the love seat, inviting her to snuggle closer to him. The light began to filter into the deck and gave his face a soft glow. Branches from the maple tree in her yard made long finger shadows across her lawn. She moved closer as his arm surrounded her then her legs shared the ottoman his feet rested on. His right arm crossed her and his hand caressed her cheek, turning her head slightly as he leaned into her for a kiss. His lips were soft yet pressing and lingered until she responded in kind.

With a sigh his left arm relaxed, "What a beautiful evening." Kate relaxed too and snuggled into the softness of his shirt. Her hair was soft in his hand and he started to stroke the long length of it. His emotion was rising, he wanted her so much. He wondered if she knew. He took one of the throw pillows that had been cast to the floor earlier and now picked one up and laid it across his lap. "Here," he said, "You can rest your head."

He loved her and wanted to say so, he wanted to be with her forever but couldn't, not now. There was another young man between them, a young man who had felt the same desire, a young man who had loved her.

He had to curb his desire and give her time. He would show her in small ways of his intent without pressing her. He would wait because the alternative was to lose her forever.

It was about four-thirty when Kate woke to the sound of a voice in the living room.

"Thanks Jacob, I'll let them know." He paused and smiled at Kate as she came into the living room, "A marriage certificate and his change of name. I can have them faxed to you today." Birdie jotted down the fax number on a small scratch pad by the phone. "All right, I'll get back to you tomorrow."

"Would you like a cup of tea or is it too early?"

"It's never too early for tea." Birdie followed Kate back to the kitchen area and closed off the living room door so they couldn't be seen from the front of the house. "Some good news though, my Mr. Bean," he waited dutifully for the giggle that followed, "will start the proceeding right away, so there is no immediate rush to have Mike go to Scotland. I will let Victoria know she will have to fax the documents she has and start to acquire a copy of Will's birth certificate.

He took the mug Kate offered him, "But, I have one more phone call to make." With that, he sat down the mug then went back into the living room searching in his jeans pocket for a crumpled piece of paper.

* * *

Alexander Cheyne was enjoying his morning brunch on the patio next to the in-ground pool. A young woman sat opposite him enjoying a coddled egg and toast. She glanced sweetly at Alex as a servant brought him a ringing phone attached to a very long extension cord.

"Robin, it's been a while," he played teasingly with the young woman's free hand, and smiled to himself. Geoffrey would take care of everything; he had trust in that, but whether Robin new of Geoffrey's own plans there was no way of telling. "How have you made out?"

Birdie wished now he could have told Alex this news in person…to see the look on his face, but satisfied himself with this, "I'm afraid I have some bad news for Geoffrey." He waited for the appropriate response. "You'll have to tell him that he won't be collecting his hefty fee after all." This was a supposition on Birdie's part but it seemed to hit home.

"I....er...what ever do you mean?"

*　　　*　　　*

Birdie could have explained but he would let the solicitors have that privilege. In the mean time Alex could just worry. The thought made him smile.

"Well, there you have it. My mission is concluded." Kate had been watching him from the kitchen and smiled at his satisfaction. "That was fun; I wish I could have seen his face."

Kate handed him his tea, "Are you sure? He can't make trouble or destroy anything?"

"He might try to steal some things, but I should think most antique items are listed somewhere and the estate money itself is safe."

The sun was beginning to give the sky a soft gray glow, but the back deck was still enclosed in relative darkness. They settled back on the love seat in a companionable silence.

Birdie raised his mug in a toast, "To us," he smiled warmly at her, "we've changed someone's life for the better."

Kate raised her mug and added to the toast, "and someone's life for the poorer."

She sat down her tea and stared at the box on

the kitchen counter that contained the separate components of the package as well as the contents of Anne Marie's boxes. William's journal lay by itself next to it. "Do you think Alex knows you are his 'kinsman' as they say?"

"Probably, that's why he sided with Geoffrey in the search. Too bad really, if he had kept quiet about the letter Jean wrote, maybe he would have kept the estate."

Kate's hand moved across his and fingered the ring he wore, "We still have a mystery though…the meaning of the rings and the table." She glanced at the journal. "Did you finish the journal?"

"Yes, but there was little else in it to explain the rings, and nothing more about the inscriptions."

He placed his hand over hers and touched the ring she now wore on the middle finger of her right hand. Kate looked up at him and smiled, "I have something to show you," she said, a hint of excitement on her face. Her bag was sitting on the floor next to the counter. Retrieving it she pulled out the note pad with the Cheyne family tree and flipped through the pages until she found what she was searching for.

Sitting back down beside Birdie she handed him the small folded piece of paper. It was the receipt for William's puzzle table. Birdie read and re-read the description.

"Not…thee Mackintosh?" He looked at Kate incredulously. "I've seen his work and I don't remember ever seeing anything like it at home." Then a funny thought struck him, "Wouldn't it be ironic if this table was at the estate and Alex has it?" He shook his head. "I wish now I hadn't called him."

Suddenly he stood up and pulled Kate up to meet his gaze. "We're going to England! Do you have a valid passport?"

Kate didn't know what to say, "Um…yes… but when?"

"As soon as I can arrange a flight," he raised a finger to stop possible protest on her part, "This is my treat." He smiled warmly at her then gave her a lingering hug then kiss. "Do you want to come with me?"

# Chapter 15

Two days and six hours later Kate and Birdie had rented a car at Heathrow Airport and were now on the road to Aylesbury some forty-five miles away. Victoria had promised to fax her information and certificates as soon as she could to Mr. Bean.

My parents live on the outskirts of the city. They're on a cruise in the Mediterranean right now, on holidays, but my Grandmother will be home as well as our housekeeper Mardie.

Birdie had his key but because he was unexpected, decided to ring the door bell so as not to startle anyone. It was a beautiful Tudor style house. The front door encased in its own stone enclosure reminded her of the little house she'd seen soldiers stand in while on guard. The upper floor of the house was painted white but had the beautiful dark wooden slats across it that made up the rectangular designs. The lower floor of the house was stone and Kate was surprised at the number of windows it held.

Mardie came to the door. Her face immediately broke out in a huge smile when she saw Birdie. "Good afternoon, Master Robin." Birdie gave her a hug and introduced Kate.

"We've come for a short visit, Mardie. Would the guest bedroom be available?"

"Gi' me a few minutes to fluff the pillows like and I'll have Geordie take the lady's bags up." She set Kate's single bag by the bottom of the staircase that ran up the side of the hallway. "Then I'm sure ye'll both be want'n a bite to eat."

"Thank you Mardie, that would be wonderful." Then in a quieter voice he asked, "How is Gran?"

Mardie's fingers played with the folds of her apron, eager to be off to the errand at hand. Kate loved her Scottish accent and wondered if she was from the north part of the country. "She's been much better this week, ask'n after you, she has. Right now she'll be asleep."

"Maybe we'll go up and see her after our tea. Right now I want to show Kate the garden." Birdie escorted Kate through the living room and out through the French doors to the garden that took up the side and back of the house.

"What a beautiful yard," she said, overwhelmed by the number of flower beds. She stood on a narrow walk that meandered its way around the garden. A gated arbor heralded the entrance to the vast beds that were scattered throughout. Most of the beds contained flowers; dahlias, and mums were the most prevalent yet were surrounded by delicate specimens that created a canvas for the brighter more vivid blooms. As you walked the cobbled path toward the back of the yard a large rose hedge divided the kitchen garden from the flower part. There was an herbal section separated from the vegetable part of the garden although Kate did notice a certain amount of integration where certain herbs were paired with certain vegetables apparently to keep pesky insects away from the crop.

"This is so beautiful, I've always wanted a garden like this." Kate held her hand out so a small lady bug larvae crawling on a stone outcrop could wriggle on to her finger then she carefully placed the black and red insect on a neighbouring plant. "How big is the property?"

Enjoying her reaction to his home he pointed to the row of trees on the far side of the property that designated their boundary line then across to the fence that enclosed the side garden. "Almost two acres. It's a lot for my father to manage but he still enjoys it. We have a gardener now which is a great help."

Just then Mardie brought out a tray and set it on the large table that stood on the patio outside the kitchen entrance. Tea and scones were served and

Kate enjoyed watching Birdie, home now in his own environment he was relaxed and comfortable in his surroundings.

After tea and a further walk around the yard they came back into the house through the kitchen; a very large space that housed two stoves, a gigantic island with butcher block top, double sink, and rows of cupboard space around the perimeter. "What a grand kitchen," exclaimed Kate, "It just makes you want to cook something!" The cook smiled at her excitement but continued without comment as she prepared a large roast of beef for the evening meal. After preparing smaller meals for the staff and elderly matron it was a pleasure to prepare a large meal again with all the trimmings.

"Let's see if Gran is up, shall we?"

Gran's room was actually a suite set to the west of the house so that it seemed like a separate apartment where she had the illusion of her privacy yet was still a permanent fixture of the family. Birdie had told Kate that his Gran had lived here ever since his parents had moved in some thirty years ago. Now of course with her degenerative condition it took more planning to attend to her needs.

Mardie had accompanied them to her rooms and left them once Birdie had called to his Grandmother.

"Come in my dear. Where have you been? I've been asking Mardie after you."

Kate noticed a slight Scottish accent, Edinburgh, she guessed. "And who might you have here?" she asked when she saw Kate.

Almost ninety she seemed in very good condition apart from the Alzheimer's condition Birdie had mentioned. Her skin was clear and her eyes had the same deep brown as Birdie's. She still had her hair and most of her own teeth and when she smiled the world seemed a happy place and Kate was glad she was able to meet the woman whose name was on the Cheyne family chart…Hannah.

Although still able to get around by herself she sat in a wheel chair usually in the afternoon which made it easier to be wheeled through the house to the main dining room area to join the family for the evening meal. Here she sat now next to a side table covered by a large draping table cloth that hung almost to the floor.

"This is Kate, Gran. She has helped me look for Connor's son." He took Kate by the arm and sat her down in a small chair across from Hannah. Kate, this is my Grandmother, Hannah McLeod." Kate took the elderly woman's hand as she sat down. Her hand was cool but firm, and she suddenly seemed fascinated by Kate's presence.

"Are you American?" she asked.

"Canadian." answered Birdie.

"I'm very pleased to meet you." Kate and Birdie had brought some of the contents of the package to her room, hoping Hannah would recognize some of the pictures. "We brought these for you to look at," she said, handing the pictures to Hannah.

Hannah retrieved her glasses from the side table and took the pictures Kate handed her. A sudden smile crossed her face as she saw the pictures. "Grandfather," she said. Kate leaned over as did Birdie and saw that she was looking at the picture of the man and woman. "Oh…and Connor, my dear Connor." She held the picture of the young man in uniform out for Birdie to see. "Have you seen Connor, then?" she asked, her eyes hopeful.

"No Gran, I'm afraid not," he said softly, he glanced at Kate with a look that said 'I'll tell her later' then held his Grandmother's hand. "We found Connor's Grandson…his name is Michael. He lives in Canada."

A sudden thought occurred to her. "My father's name was Michael," she said. "Father didn't approve you know …" Then she turned toward the side table and lifted a large gold framed picture. It was an old photograph of a young man standing with his buddies in front of and on a tank, a tank crew. It was obviously taken during the war and appeared to be in the African desert. Her eyes grew soft and she held the picture close to her breast, then she smiled, "He'll be home soon now, the war is almost over." She turned the picture toward Kate for her to see. "Here's Thomas, he's in the Scots Greys," she said pointing to the young man on the far right. He was young, thought Kate, then, they all were during the war. His hair was fair and he smiled dutifully as did his buddies for the shot. A handsome young man, not unlike Evan. They were dead now, killed during the invasion of Italy in 1944. Kate blinked to keep the tears that were forming at bay. Hannah placed the picture back on the table and smiled at her young husband. "I miss him so much. He hasn't seen the baby yet." At this moment Hannah was content in her past.

Then she looked as if she suddenly saw Birdie and was pulled back to the present. "I'm so glad you're home Robin."

"I'll leave you the pictures we found then I'll come back before supper and tell you more." With that Birdie gave her a hug and kiss then took Kate's hand as they left his grandmother with her memories.

"She likes you," whispered Birdie as they left her room. "You can see though how her thoughts get mixed up…"

Kate wasn't listening, she was thinking of Thomas, dead now over sixty years and Hannah who was still waiting for him to come home. When her mind was right she must have lived a lonely life, longing for the man she had loved and couldn't have. Would that be Kate's fate as well? She thought of Evan's picture now on her bedside table, the number of nights she cried herself to sleep, she didn't want to end up like Hannah, alone for the rest of her life yearning for someone who could never come back.

Suddenly Kate couldn't hold the tears back. She turned toward Birdie and buried her head in the warmth of his shirt. She liked this man and realized now that she had resisted her feelings because of guilt, now she held him tight and began to sob. Birdie didn't know what to say so just held her, stroking her hair until she was able to speak. Kate felt the muscular arms about her and squeezed her grip around his waist. "I don't want to be alone," she whispered, "I'm tired of living in the past, I want to be with you."

Kate looked up at Birdie, tears streaming down her face. A wave of understanding and tenderness crossed his face and he smiled back softly at her, wiping the tears away from her cheeks with a free hand, he kissed her gently. "I love you…I have from the moment I first met you." he said softly.

Kate couldn't think, she was here and now, and loved this man. They stood for several more moments embraced in each others arms kissing.

"Look, you'll want to rest. Why don't you go to your room and freshen up, maybe have a nap and I'll call you for supper." Kate nodded, afraid to speak in case the happiness spilled out. She was in love with Birdie. She knew it now.

Birdie took her to her room; his heart was pounding so hard that he thought Kate could hear it. He gave her another lingering kiss and then went to retrieve the rest of the package contents before returning to his Grandmother's suite.

Supper was late but it was still light outside. The roast beef was just as Kate hoped it would be with roasted potatoes and Yorkshire pudding. Home grown vegetables and luscious gravy completed the meal. Custard pastries were served shortly after.

The room was grand, dark woodwork covering three of the walls while floor length windows faced the back yard garden. Their table easily sat eight and the three diners sat together at the kitchen end of the room.

Hannah had joined them and for the moment seemed in this world. Birdie had sat with her for a few hours and they had talked about everything he had discovered. She had had a moment's distress when she learned that her brother had died young but rebounded later once she realized that his grandson would be coming to visit her.

Kate enjoyed watching Birdie interact with his Grandmother. He was kind and caring and she was happy for him. Happy that he was now able to discuss his family with Hannah, that it wasn't too late after all.

Kate suddenly had a thought and took Hannah's hand in hers. "Do you ever remember seeing a table with cats on it?"

A smile instantly covered her face, "I remember my mother had a kitty cat table," she replied, suddenly distracted from reality. "I was never allowed to sit at the table when I was colouring my pictures. I told her I would be careful but she told me it was special."

She sighed then gave a little pout, "I would have been very careful, I liked the small kitties. Mother always kept the table covered with a long tablecloth. She said it was special and must always stay in the family." She gave Kate a wistful look, "I would have been careful."

"I'm sure you would have been very careful," agreed Kate. She glanced at Birdie who nodded slightly. "Do you know where your mother's table is now?" she asked.

"My mother has it, but she won't let you sit at the table either. She keeps it near her in her bedroom now."

Kate smiled warmly at the older woman and patted her hand. Hannah had begun to close her eyes and the days' excitement was obviously tiring for her.

Mardie came into the dining room just in time and prepared to wheel Hannah back to her room and help prepare her for bed. Kate rose and gave Hannah a hug goodnight.

"We'll see you tomorrow," she said.

Alone in the large dining room Kate sat next to Birdie who stood at the head of the table moving his chair enough for the wheelchair to pass by. He slumped back down in his chair. He smiled at Kate and took her hand in his. "Have I told you in the last half hour that I love you?"

He looked tired after a day of traveling. "Yes, every ten minutes actually."

He came to the back of Kate's chair and put his arms around her then nuzzled her neck. Her body responded and melted back toward him. He wanted to feel Kate next to him, to explore her to have her beside him forever, he couldn't wait, but for now he would have to. He would have to wait until Kate felt the same.

"It's been a long day." Kate put her hands on

his, “I know it’s still early but I can’t keep my eyes open.”

“I’ll see you tomorrow.” Birdie pulled Kate’s chair out for her. He walked her to her bedroom door. Her arms reached around his neck as Kate drew him nearer. She looked into his eyes. They were smiling at her with a reflected happiness. Kate felt his arms tighten around her. She felt his soft day-old beard as his lips kissed her cheek, then teasingly brushed her lips as he kissed the other cheek. Kate’s arms locked behind his head and she redirected his lips to hers where they lingered in a deep passionate kiss, his tongue exploring her mouth invitingly.

“Good night,” she said, her eyes not leaving his. She released her grip and he took her hands in his and kissed them. “I love you.”

“I love you too.” His smile broadened and he glanced at her bedroom door, suggestively.

“Good night.” She smiled back, “I’ll see you tomorrow,” and left him in the hall as she closed her door.

# Chapter 16

Tomorrow for Kate came at eleven o'clock in the morning. She had been tired. By the time she showered and dressed it was close to dinner time. Mardie was milling around the house attending to the duties of a housekeeper.

She passed Kate as she came down the stairs, "Dinner will be served at twelve-thirty in the dining room, Miss."

"Thank you, has …Robin come down yet?"

"Aye, Miss, he's been gone since early this morning, but I'll expect he'll be back in time for the midday meal."

The morning was sunny and it promised to be a beautiful day. With dinner almost ready Kate decided to spend a few minutes in the garden off the dining room. She sat in the love seat of a wicker patio set facing the door so she could see when Birdie came back.

The events of the previous day had kept Kate awake long after midnight. She was so happy she thought she would burst. She couldn't wait to tell Kelly. Her sister could stop arranging supper dates for her now, she had found someone, yet there were so many unknowns. Would they continue a long distance relationship? That didn't seem doable, as his home was here and hers back in Canada. What would his parents think?

Then there was the question of the table; that alone had taken up a good hour of contemplation. Was it at the estate under Alex's nose on display as a valued antique or hidden in some attic under heavy sheets to keep it clean? Where would the family have kept Jean's things? She thought of Anne Marie's possessions stored in the attic of Yvonne Lyonne for years and would still be there if she hadn't decided to search for Connor Cheyne.

Kate wondered if there was an attic in this house full of old unwanted things? She would ask Mardie next time she saw her. "Well, hello." A small fuzzy bumble bee hovered in front of her for a moment as if deciding whether she was a flower or not then buzzed away to a near by red bloom in the bed nearest her.

Her heart leapt at Birdie's arrival home. He came through the living room and met her in the garden. "Hello, my love." He was beaming. He gave her a warm hug and kiss. "I have some good news." He joined Kate on the love seat. "Well, good for Mike, I mean. Jacob has begun the legal proceedings and it should be all finalized by mid September. Victoria has ordered her husband's birth certificate and Jacob should have it within the week." He sighed as if a huge weight had been taken off his shoulders. "In a way I'm a little sorry it's all over. I love a good hunt and this was fun…and if Gran hadn't sent that package I would never have met you."

Mardie came to the dining room door indicating that dinner was served. It was a buffet style meal with salad, salmon fishcakes, poached eggs, toast and asparagus.

Hannah had her mid day meal as usual in her room and it was just the two of them seated at the large oak table. "Do you think your parents would know if there were any of Jean's possessions stored here?" she asked suddenly after sitting down with her plate of food.

"They might, but all the years I've lived here I don't' recall anyone mentioning the subject. Oh, I suddenly forgot…" The housekeeper came in to add fresh tea to the service, "Mardie, how is Alexis?"

"She'll be doing fine, Master Robin."

"Excuse me Dear, I have to call her, she may still be on break." Birdie left most of his plate untouched as he rose and left Kate.

"Mardie," The housekeeper stopped her

fussing and turned toward Kate. "Are there storage areas in this house that might be big enough to store a table? Maybe a table, so big?" Kate showed the rough dimensions with her hands. Mardie knew every inch of the house and if anyone knew of stored items it would be her.

"Just the attic, Miss, and a small room off the basement."

"Thank you, Mardie. Yes, please." Kate lifted her cup in response to the offered tea.

Birdie wasn't gone long, just enough to touch base with Alexis. He was back and if his food had cooled it didn't seem to matter. "She's fine now, and as I thought is back to work." He tried one of the asparagus, and dipped it into the poached egg before biting off the end, "She can't wait to meet you."

Kate had finished her meal and was finishing up her tea, "Mardie says there is some storage in the attic and in the basement. Do you think we should check those for Jean's table?"

"It seems a good place to start. I asked Alexis if she knew where exactly Mum and Dad had gone." He smiled, "Somewhere on a river cruise, she said. And as usual they never take their phones with them when they go on holidays, so I can't call and ask them." Birdie finished up the last of his fish cake with an appreciative sigh. "So we might as well take a look around ourselves, they won't be back for another week."

The attic had a staircase entrance that ran along the west end of the top floor and was easy enough to get to. Walking among the numerous boxes, bags and furniture was a different matter. Like most storage areas it was crammed with non-essential items as well as cherished remnants of the past. It wasn't as dusty as Kate expected and actually quite cool considering it was still August. There was an automatic exhaust fan that blew out the hotter air as the thermostat reached a certain temperature.

There were trunks of old memorabilia and clothing that Kate would loved to have looked through but they were searching for a table at the moment and family relics could wait. It took almost an hour for the two of them to search the attic. Some of the attic contents had undoubtedly belonged to Jean but there was no sign of a table. Perhaps later they would have to revisit the idea of going through all the boxes of paper in search of a clue but for now they would head down to the basement storage room.

Mardie passed them on the stairs as they hurriedly made their way downstairs to the basement. The room was quite small and a little musty smelling, obviously not as well ventilated as the attic. It didn't take long to discover that this room housed a different category of items; Christmas decorations, flower pots and soil, mason jars for canning and a vast assortment of sporting equipment. No table.

"I didn't think we'd actually find it after all these years," confessed Birdie. "If anywhere it's probably at the manor house. Let's just hope Alex doesn't realize its worth."

They came back up to the main floor as Mardie was clearing away the dinner dishes. She smiled when she saw them together hand in hand. Birdie thanked her as they passed then went out to the back garden with Kate. There was a small potting shed near the herb garden where they washed their dusty hands after their search. Birdie stole another kiss then escorted Kate to a long garden couch at the far end of the patio nearer the kitchen. It was sunny now and a lot warmer. This part of the garden was sheltered by a pergola that filtered the afternoon sun for those seated below. The synthetic rattan couch was large and easily allowed Kate to stretch out; her head resting on a folded blanket laid across Birdie's lap.

"Where did Jean live after Connor's Grandfather died?"

"I don't really know, probably with Hannah somewhere. It wouldn't have been at Cheyne Manor." Birdie fanned out Kate's hair on the blanket behind her head. She was deep in thought but didn't mind Birdie running his fingers through her hair. It felt relaxing.

"What a shame that's the one thing Hannah remembers about the table; that she wasn't allowed to sit at it. It must have been important for Jean to keep it covered."

Kate reached back and took the hand that was stroking her hair and placed it under her neck. The hand found a new interest and began to softly stroke her neck and face. It wavered slightly as it moved to more alluring areas and Kate gently repositioned it, her hand on his.

"You of all people should know what children are like," he commented, "You write children's books...you must have come across a few of them." Then he laughed, "But you're right, it is sad she only has that memory."

Almost choked by Birdie's hand as she sat up abruptly, Kate now had another thought.

"Jean kept it covered up all the time, Hannah said, with a long table cloth." She waited for Birdie to agree. "When did Jean die?"

"Sometime in the nineties, I'm not exactly sure of the date." Kate was excited and Birdie wasn't sure where she was going with this.

"Hannah had the package and the letter that

she was keeping for her mother yet she had forgotten about them all these years. What if she had other things that belonged to her mother and also forgot where they had come from or what they were?"

Birdie grabbed her hand and pulled her up from the couch, "The covered table in Gran's room?"

"It's worth a look."

"I don't believe I've ever seen that table uncovered, it's been in that very spot for as long as I can remember." Then he shook his head, "My parents must have noticed it surely, though they wouldn't know much about it." Birdie checked his watch, "Gran should be napping now maybe we can go in quietly and check."

They entered the room quietly leaving the light off less it be seen from the adjoining bedroom. Kate was so excited by their hunt that Birdie let her lead the way. Carefully Kate removed the picture of Thomas, a box of tissue, a glass of water and the shaded lamp that lit the surrounding area. The table cloth was not the usual kind of covering one found on tables. This one seemed to be especially made for the table.

The table itself was a rectangular shape but had its corners cut at a forty five degree angle giving the table four long and four short flat faces around the edge. The table cloth had been cut and stitched to hug these corners tightly thus ensuring the decorative covering would not slip off. Kate lifted the one corner of the cloth revealing the front two table legs. Mackintosh's style could be seen in the plain splayed legs that were wide at the bottom then narrowed as they reached the top. The quartersawn oak gave the wood its tiger striped look. Kate took the cloth off completely and found another softer pad that covered the table top surface, it had a plastic lining that would further protect the table from moisture. "What a beautiful table," admired Kate. Birdie helped her lift the table away from Hannah's recliner then set it out in the centre of the room to look at. It was heavy for a small table and looked identical from all sides except the front where a small drawer took up one of the longer faces of the table. The table top itself was about six inches in height and gave the drawer enough space for storing larger objects such as books or journals.

"What do you think?" asked Kate, glowing with the result of their discovery.

"I've never seen it before." He touched the striped wood and the smooth edge of the surface. "It is beautiful and I can see why Jean didn't want it marked or scratched, although I doubt oak would scratch easily. But look at the inlays, they're brass."

The wood was stained dark and had numerous

inch sized brass inlays across its surface.

"Look… they're cats!" Kate whispered excitedly. "Oh, Birdie, we've found it."

There was a stifled snore in Hannah's room, "Let's take it to your room, I don't want to wake her."

Together they carried the table upstairs to Kate's room where it stood on the rug before them as they sat on her bed and contemplated their discovery.

Birdie opened the drawer and found a stamp, a silver brush and comb set and a linen handkerchief. "Nothing here."

Kate moved to the floor so she could study the brass inlays closer. "From the front everything looks symmetrical, but the back has no brass inlays on the legs, just the top and sides." Her hand ran over the brass; smooth and cool under her fingers.

"Okay, we have the messages from the rings," said Birdie replacing the front drawer. "The cats show the way…Your fate hides within…and…Your mother holds the key."

Kate smoothed her hand over the table top and along the flat edges, "There doesn't appear to be a key hole anywhere, even on the drawer." Then she sat back and looked at the cats. Kate fingered the cats one by one, "I wonder why there are some on the front legs and not on the back, then there are more on the surface towards the back."

Birdie looked at the ring on his finger then at the brass cats on the front legs. They were mirror images of each other but didn't look exactly as the cat on the ring did. These were pointing upwards, towards the next set at the top of the legs, these too pointed upwards. On the outer edge of the flat table top just above the front legs, two rows of cats made their way towards the centre, each pointing to its adjacent neighbour until coming to a stop at the centre where one cat seemed to join the two trails of cats.

"Look at this one." Kate was pointing to the central cat. "It's different! It isn't pointing; it's just sitting with its front feet in front of it." She looked at Birdie, puzzled. "That's strange."

"Well, it is a puzzle table, don't forget."

"I've seen a puzzle table once before where you press something and it opens," offered Kate. She reached out and pressed the centre brass cat but nothing happened.

"Look at the cats behind it…they're not pointing towards the middle cat like the front ones are." Birdie traced the two trails of cats that like the front two fanned out toward the back and ended just above the back legs of the table, only this time they were pointing toward the back legs away from the centre cat. They both moved to the back of the table and saw that unlike the front of the table there were no brass cats on the back legs; they had stopped at the two shorted faces of the top and each cat like the centre cat was sitting, its paws down.

"Well, this is interesting." said Birdie as he rechecked the cat in the centre of the table top and compared it with the two inlays along the back-side of the table. "They're the same!"

Kate reached over and pressed the two cats simultaneously. Birdie waited but nothing happened. "Maybe we should press all three at the same time," she suggested.

"All right, you press the center one and I'll take care of the sides." They tried repeatedly and again with no success. "This might take a while, I have to find Mardie."

Birdie left to find the housekeeper. He suggested she bring another table up stairs for his Grandmother before she woke up and then straighten up the room so as not to distress her. Acknowledging this rather odd request Mardie went off to find a suitable replacement.

Birdie was back shortly and found Kate sitting on her bed staring at the table, lost in thought. "There's something in the table," she started, "but we can't break it because it too might be valuable." She ran her hand across the top once more, "William went to a great deal of trouble having this made so there must be a way in. It has to be the three cats; the other cats are pointing to them."

"I tend to agree with you. Maybe there's something underneath the table top we have to push." Birdie got down on the carpet and peered up under the table.

"Are there any cats there?" asked Kate.

"No, nothing out of the ordinary." He got back up and sat down on the bed next to Kate.

Kate was glad Birdie had closed the bedroom door because now they could hear Mardie downstairs as she carried a small table to his Grandmother's room. "Goodness knows what she is thinking." said Birdie a little sheepishly, "I didn't want to say too much." Birdie looked at the bed they were sharing and smiled.

Kate shook her head slightly and smiled, "I'm sure my reputation will be safe, Mardie seems like a very discreet person."

"She is…very." Then thinking better of it Birdie turned his attention back to the table.
He studied the wood around the brass cat. "The middle inlay doesn't seem as if it would move, but why is that one prominent?"

Kate used her hand to get a rough measure, "It appears to be exactly in the centre, can you see the centre from the bottom?"

"No, it's completely closed in." Birdie pulled the drawer open again then removed it completely from its enclosure. "Maybe, from inside the drawer opening." Birdie turned the table toward the window so the opening could be better seen. He reached inside the vacated space and felt around. Besides the drawer cleats there was nothing extra along the sides. There was a backing behind the drawer area that divided the table roughly in half.

With his hand further back now he tried to judge where the centre cat might be above his hand.

Then he felt it, a lever. Birdie smile triumphantly, "I've got something, a small lever of some sort on the wooden backing." He retrieved his hand and let Kate feel the metal lever. It was attached to the dividing wall inside the table top and just below the central cat.

"Should I try it?" Birdie could see she was dying to see what would happen if she pulled it.

"Try it, but don't pull hard, just see if it will move without a lot of pressure."

Excited by their find Kate did as Birdie suggested, but the lever would not move.

"It won't move," Kate tried again, "I don't want to break it." She removed her hand from the drawer opening and took up her seat again next to Birdie.

"Okay, there's a lever below the centre cat and

we can't get behind the side cats because the table bottom is solidly enclosed." She stood up and went again to the back cats that sat as if waiting for them to figure it out. Kate touched the two brass cats, like the top cat they too were solid in their wooden space. "What if we tried pressing them while you pull the lever?"

"We can try that." Birdie got back down on the carpet and reached back into the drawer space where his hand found the small lever. "Say when."

Kate put each of her hands on a brass cat and gently pushed, "Now," she said hesitantly. Birdie tried to move the lever and was rewarded with a clicking sound.

"Oh!" The long back-side of the table top popped down toward her catching her off balance. Hinged from the inside it now revealed a plain oak board across the back. It had a smaller drawer front built into it. It was an ingenious design; the whole long side could be covered up by the beautiful tiger striped wood once it was raised and clicked back into place.

Birdie joined her and stared at the back of the table. "Imagine, William designing this." He examined the workmanship, "You can't even tell the back panel opens up."

Kate smiled at their success and pointed to

their find. "There's the meaning of the third ring… Your mother holds the key." This smaller drawer required a small key of some kind. "You don't know how to pick a lock, do you?" asked Kate dubiously.

"I have a great many skills but unfortunately never had occasion to learn." He smiled at Kate, "You should be pleased about that, you know." Then a thought occurred to him, a lock smith could be hired but only as a very last resort.

"Your mother holds the key, whose mother?" thought Kate out loud.

"Maybe Lydia, or Jean," offered Birdie.

"Maybe, but William wanted his Grandson Connor to find this so it was probably Jean he was referring to. Jean had lived with Hannah, and unless Hannah has lost it, the key should be with her."

"It could also be up in the attic with some of Jean's things too," suggested Birdie.

Kate brushed her hair back out of her eyes, "Let's try Hannah first."

# Chapter 17

They'd spent most of the afternoon in Kate's bedroom studying the table and now it was close to supper time. They had closed the secret cover and placed the table cloth back over the table and now went down to Hannah's suite to check on the replacement table Mardie had set up. It was about the same size and although covered with a different tablecloth didn't look that out of place once the former table's items had been neatly arranged back in their place.

They took up usual seats at the dining table and waited for Hannah to join them. Once Hannah had arrived and Birdie helped her to get settled, Mardie signaled the cook to begin supper. Together they enjoyed roast lamb with rosemary and boiled potatoes with mint sauce.

Birdie found it hard to keep his eyes off of Kate. He loved how she tried to engage his Grandmother in conversation and whether it was the past or present, Kate took an interest in her stories. As casual as this seemed Birdie also realized where she was heading; he like her was eager to resume their search. They would have to speak to Hannah about it so if Kate could casually introduce the subject while keeping his Gran from any stress he was for that.

Dessert was chocolate cake with chocolate icing. "Mother used to make chocolate cake every Saturday," reminisced Hannah, "She knew it was my favourite." The elderly woman smiled warmly at Kate. "Have you met my mother yet?"

"Not yet," Kate answered as she realized Hannah was her young self again. "But Robin has told me about her." She looked at Robin and he nodded slightly, "She had a special key that she gave you to look after."

The elderly woman brightened at the mention of her mother's trust in her. "Yes, it was a special key…I am never suppose to loose it."

Birdie smiled at his Grandmother and took her hand in his, "May we see the key, Gran?"

Back to reality she looked at her Grandson fondly, "Of course, Robin. Will you bring your young lady too?"

"Yes Gran, right after we finish our tea."

It was another half hour before supper was concluded and Mardie wheeled Hannah back to her suite with Kate and Birdie following. "I'll be up in half an hour Mum and help ye to bed."

"Thank you, Mardie," said Birdie.

Kate took the small seat opposite Hannah and waited for Birdie to ask about the key.

The current table with the portrait of Thomas filled the space nicely and Hannah didn't seem to have noticed the change.

"Gran, do you have your mother's key here?"

She looked surprised then pulled a chain from around her neck. "I always wear the key," she said. "Mother said the key must stay safe." She fingered the golden coloured key that hung from a chain around her neck.

"May I see it, Gran?" She was hesitant for a moment then pulled the chain over her head and handed it to Birdie. It was a small brass key and looked the size that might fit the lock they had found.

"You must be careful, Robin, mother will be angry if you lose it."

He gave her a gentle hug, "I won't lose it. I'll be right back." He motioned to Kate, then the two of them left and ran upstairs to her room.

"I hope this will work!" Birdie said as he took his place on the floor beneath the table. Kate stood ready to press the two brass cats when he gave the word. "Okay, now!"

The hidden door sprung open again revealing the hidden drawer with the key hole exposed. Birdie held the brass key to the lock then tried to insert the blade into the keyway. It went in but Birdie could tell it was too small to be effective. "No, it's not the right key, it's too small." He looked disappointed and gave Kate a weak smile. "We better take it back."

He handed the key to Kate to look at. She held the key up to the light. "I have a key like this," she commented after fingering the key. It fits into my jewellery box

"Come on. Let's see."

After they closed up the secret panel, Birdie took her hand and again ran back down the stairs to Hannah's room. Kate took her former spot while Birdie stood next to Hannah and handed the chain back to her. "Thank you, Gran." He glanced at Kate and thought he would try her suggestion. "Gran, do you have a jewellery box."

"My Mother's jewellery box?" Hannah seemed distressed for a moment as she tried to recall where her mother's box was. "I was supposed to keep it safe," she said. "Where did she put it?"

"Maybe it was with the package you sent to Connor," offered Kate.

"The closet in my bedroom, perhaps." she said.

"I'll check," said Birdie, and he left them to check the closet in Hannah's bedroom.

The closet was a walk in and housed most of Hannah's unused clothing, along with shoes, books, small boxes and blankets. Along the back wall behind a box of boots Birdie found a cream coloured vinyl jewellery box. It was locked.

Hurriedly Birdie reached up and pulled the box down from the shelf it was on. It had a slight coating of dust and appeared to have been sitting there for a very long time. Birdie would be sure not to mention that to Mardie.

Kate was entertaining Hannah with stories of her childhood as Birdie came back in with the jewellery box. "That's the kind I had when I was little." Kate said as she passed the box to Hannah.

"Shall we try your key, Gran?" Hannah handed the key to Birdie and with a gentle pat on Kate's hand he tried the small key. It turned and the lid was lifted up, Hannah leaned forward to view the contents along with Birdie and Kate. The lid had little hooks that held the necklaces and a small oval mirror. There were two rectangular storage areas in the bottom that housed bracelets, brooches and ear rings. Down the centre was a rippled row of velvet that allowed rings to be wedged in creases between the raised parts. All the creases held rings, all but one which held a key, a dark metal key slightly larger than the key they had tried in the table earlier.

"There it is," said Hannah, relieved now that she had found her mother's key. She held the key up for Birdie to inspect.

"May I borrow it?" asked Birdie, "I'll bring it back right away."

Mardie came to the door just then ready to help Hannah get ready for bed. Hannah held the key up for Birdie to take.

Once again Kate and Birdie were back up the stairs to her room. Birdie took his place ready to move the latch as Kate pressed the brass cats. Once again the cover door popped open revealing the hidden drawer. "Well, here goes," said Birdie and he slipped the blade into the keyway. It fit and he turned the bow of the key until… it clicked.

He pulled the drawer open slowly and kept pulling until the drawer came out altogether. A yellowed folded piece of paper covered the contents. Birdie carefully took this out and handed it to Kate. Below the paper were two small bags. Made of a rough woven unbleached cotton they also had dulled with time. Birdie took the drawer over to the bed and the two of them sat on either side, hesitant to touch the contents. These bags had remained hidden for so long, placed there by his Great, Great Grandfather. Birdie wanted to treasure the moment.

"What does the letter say?" he asked Kate.

She gently unfolded the paper. It was addressed on the outside to "***My Kinsman***".

Birdie picked up the smaller of the two bags. He felt the small items roll beneath his fingers as he moved them through the bag. He looked expectantly at Kate. Then he pulled the worn drawstring open and poured the contents into his hand.

Kate gasped then stared at Birdie. They looked like small pebbles, some clearer than others, with irregular shapes they reminded Kate of ice after it had been chiseled with an ice pick and broken up unto smaller pieces. "Are those what I think they are?"

Birdie looked dazed and carefully cupped a second hand around the first in case he dropped them. "Diamonds, uncut diamonds." He gently placed the stones back inside the bag, then picked up the second bag which felt twice as heavy.

A shiver ran through him as he suddenly realized the enormity of their discovery.
Instead of feeling elated he felt…scared. Kate saw his face and put her hand on his. "Let's read the letter," she suggested.

*I hope this letter is found by a Kinsman. For if you have read my journal and found the meaning of the rings you are indeed a Kinsman of mine.*

*Do not be afraid of the table's contents but do*

*be afraid of what they can do, for greed is a dangerous thing.*

*I can tell you now that these diamonds were stolen by thieves and these same thieves were killed by me when I was attacked by them. I retrieved the bags from them and as it is very difficult to find an owner of a fortune I decided not to try. They have been with me ever since that day and I have treasured them for what they have brought me.*

"Those two thieves must be the miners who tried to kill William in South Africa." said Birdie.

*Be warned my friend and tell no one of their existence and use them sparingly so as not to cause unwanted attention. For years I have had an association with a gem merchant in Paris a Monsieur Henri Boulanger. His son was learning the trade at that time and may still be involved today. I would suggest you acquire a bank account in both France and Switzerland to help with transactions.*

*As to my story, you have read much of it in my journal, the rest is as follows. After the war was over I returned home. I made a trip to France in search of a merchant I could trust. I went to see Lydia who had gone to her Aunt's in Paris and she alone I told of my ordeal and good fortune. I returned to Scotland with enough money to buy some land near Pitlochry in Perthshire and began to build my home. I waited for*

*Lydia to return from France, and her father suddenly having no objection to our marriage gave his consent. It took several years and a few trips to Monsieur Boulanger's office before I finally completed our home. But I always made sure to use the wealth of the stones sparingly. I have helped a few of my friends; soldiers who had been with me during the war, but I was always careful not to flaunt my wealth.*

*You must do the same, please always remember this as it will keep you and your family safe from greed...greed and jealously of others.*

*You must develop a cover story to explain money you suddenly have that does not seem too beyond belief. It will be difficult not to leave a paper trail.*

*My friend, I wish I had met you, but we may finally meet one day and you can tell me then if there were stones enough to leave to your sons and daughters.*

*Farewell Kinsman*

Tears had suddenly filled Kate's eyes and she carefully folded the letter back along the aged lines of the paper. Her arms reached out to Birdie and he gave her a firm hug.

"I had the same feeling for a moment," he said in a whisper, "when I opened the pouch and saw them. I suddenly felt what he meant when he said...

the greed and jealously of others."

"We must be careful," he said finally, and put the bags back into the drawer then took the drawer back to its hiding place in the table. Birdie replaced the letter as well then closed up the cover as it sprung back into place. "I'll have to find another key for Gran to put back into the jewellery box, this one is too valuable…too dangerous."

He came back to Kate and taking her hands lifted her up. "Don't be afraid. It will all be okay; I know how to be careful." then he smiled, "It's what I do." He took Kate in his arms and kissed her tenderly.

After a lengthy hug Kate sat back down on the bed, "So now what?" she asked a little nervous.

Birdie grinned broadly, "We go to Paris!"

# Chapter 18

It was just after seven in the morning and the Cheyne Manor was coming to life. The gardener began the fall cleanup in the flower beds while the groundskeeper made his rounds of the property. The new owner of the manor house had wished to keep things as they were for the moment but wanted to have an update regarding the vast property's resources.

It would be an extensive list; there were two hundred and eighty acres of land to account for, stables, two cottages, a pond and woodlands. Live stock was minimal yet diverse; a few dozen sheep, four horses, and numerous chickens, ducks and a large dog left behind by the previous occupant.

Cheyne Manor now belonged to a new owner and the groundskeeper was glad. There had been too many things neglected by Duncan Cheyne and his son Alexander. They had been difficult men to work for and their lack of care for the property had bothered the groundskeeper. He had been in the estates employ for almost forty-five years and had a love for the property and was glad now that the new owners were delighted with the estate and now that they were legally the owners and not subject to the rules of the trust, they could enjoy the lands as they were meant to be enjoyed. They would care for the land.

They were a nice young couple he thought, the wife finally joining her husband from Canada, after he had a chance to move some of their things in. The manor house was furnished of course but he was sure the wife would appreciate the decor and make few changes at first. She seemed impressed with the premises yet a little overwhelmed at the size of the house. It had six bedrooms, four full bathrooms, two WCs an extra large kitchen area and four large comfortable rooms on the main floor that could be used as sitting room, drawing room, living room, or dining room.

The Manor house had a full staff as well and he hoped the new owners would be able to support a staff of that size. He had no idea of the young couple's financial status but would be saddened if some of the staff had to leave. He'd known most of them for many years and all of them, he knew, loved Cheyne Manor.

He made his way over to the stables and nodded good morning to the stable man. "How is Barney this mornin'?" he asked the younger man as he entered the century old barn.

"He's mending well says the doctor. He's a braw laddie."

"Aye, he is that." agreed the groundskeeper. "Ye'll be watchin' him closely then."

Satisfied that the horse's injury was being monitored he continued his walk toward the main kitchen garden. He walked through the walled garden gate and was greeted by the large Airedale. "'ere Bruce." He knelt down and gave the dog an affectionate tousle.

The cook had a liking for the large animal too and always made sure he was fed properly. The groundskeeper was glad, he enjoyed walking the woods with the dog.

The cook Annie, saw him and gave a good morning wave. "Hae thay come doon yet?" he asked. He noticed it was nearly nine o'clock and the young couple had not yet developed a routine for rising on time for breakfast.

"Och, tis no a problem, they're a bonnie couple." The groundskeeper had noticed the same feeling among all the staff. They were happier, more confident and enjoying the new owners.

The house keeper, Mrs. Walker came in through the dining room to check on breakfast. "They're down now, Annie." She turned to go back into the dining room then added. "They should be arriving around four o'clock, Annie, so tea for seven people. I think sandwiches would be welcome, I'm sure they'll be wanting a bite to eat after their flight."

The cook nodded, "Tis all arranged, Mum" With that the house keeper returned to her tasks in the dining room.

*　　　*　　　*

It was later in the afternoon that she stood by her bedroom window and once again checked the lane way that led from the main road to the parking area of Cheyne Manor.

She chose this room because it gave the best view. It was just after three o'clock and she was getting anxious, if they landed on time at one-thirty she figured it wouldn't take longer than ninety minutes to get here from Glasgow.

"They're here!" she called then, ran down the stairs hoping to be the first to greet the leading car that came up the lane way.

Mike Lyonne's family was in the first car. He got out and took his young child in his arms so his wife could get out of the backseat where she had been sitting with her daughter.

Birdie had reached the car first. He smiled broadly as he took Mike's hand in greeting, "Welcome Cousin. We thought maybe you gotten lost."

"Impossible," laughed Mike. "There aren't that many roads to begin with and once you get on one you can't get off." The woman in the back seat came and stood by the two men straightening her skirt. "This is my wife, Danielle," he said before handing the little girl to his wife, "and Meg"

Danielle, a little weary after such a long flight, smiled at Birdie. "It's nice to finally meet you." She looked around at the surrounding buildings and grounds. "So this is Cheyne Manor?"

Birdie smiled at her reaction, "It's a bit overwhelming, isn't it?"

Kate caught up to Birdie just in time to hear the family introductions, and she smiled at the pretty little girl who had her mother's fair hair. "…and this is my wife, Kate," said Birdie.

"Hello, Danielle, nice to see you again. How was your flight?"

Danielle smiled at her young daughter, "As well as can be expected traveling with a little monkey like this one." and she released her grip on the struggling little girl who wanted to get down and chase a white duck she had just spotted near the stable.

Kate and Danielle had met twice at Victoria's while Mike was taking care of legal matters in Scotland.

"A pleasure to finally meet you in person, Mike." she said looking at the two men standing side by side. This was the first time she had seen Mike. They had spoken numerous times on the phone to plan this trip with Kelly and Ted but now she looked at him with renewed interest...they could have been brothers, they looked so much alike.

The second car finally came into view and slowly parked next to Mike's car in the parking area. Kelly stepped out first and shook her coat free of wrinkles made after sitting for so long. "Kelly, Ted! I'm so glad to see you. I thought you'd never get here!" Kate hugged her sister then Ted.

"Oh my," said Kelly after she had taken in the immenseness of the house from close up. It looked like a castle from a fairy tale. The exterior walls were covered in white harling and the dressing of dark gray sandstone gave them a crenellation effect. The house was symmetrical and the main entrance way looked like a small version of a castle gatehouse. "So this is Cheyne Manor. It didn't look that big in the picture you sent," she shook her head slightly then, she smiled, "So, do you like living in Scotland?"

"Very much, I like everything about it, especially the husband."

"You know the family is still a little miffed at you for eloping in Paris." She looked around the grounds then glanced at Birdie who had scarcely taken his eyes off Kate as she welcomed Kelly and Ted. "But I guess I can't blame you. Besides it gives us a place to go on vacation."

Kelly reached for Kate's left hand, "Let's have a look." She fingered the gold ring on Kate's hand. Birdie had designed the ring for her; a cat based upon the Sutherland crest but where the cats on the three other rings all held up their empty paw, this one held up a diamond, a discrete moderate sized diamond. "It's beautiful."

Ted had joined the rest of their company while Danielle and Meg had wandered around the gardens that edged the drive way. Meg was splashing her fingers in the fountain and giggled as the water hit her face with a cool spray.

Ted hadn't asked many questions after realizing that Geoffrey hadn't arrived in Vancouver. His business associates had called Ted two days later asking if he had intended to send his photographer. Ted had liked Geoffrey but also had a sense that Geoffrey marched to his own tune so hadn't been surprised that the photographer had gotten side tracked. Instead Ted had told his people to get another photographer and hadn't thought too much of it afterwards. Now after hearing Kate's story about the missing heir he was sorry he hadn't told her but then, he thought, maybe things would have turned out differently if she had known earlier. He looked around the well manicured gardens and the beautiful old home and was glad things had turned out the way they had.

The stable man came over to the group and addressed Birdie, "Shall I be takin' the bags up, Sir?"

"Thank you, Cam. You can ask Mrs. Walker, she'll know which rooms to use."

Birdie turned to address his guests, "Tea will be served at four o'clock, but for now go up and get settled and we'll see you shortly."

Tea began shortly after four and after a freshening up their guests joined them in the main dining room. Tea or coffee was offered along with scones, sandwiches and small meat filled pastries. Annie had prepared a tray of finger sized desserts as well. Danielle had helped Annie prepare a bottle for Meg who was currently curled up in a comfortable winged chair in the corner of the room, sound asleep

Birdie and Mike had adjourned to talk business and catch up on the proposal Birdie had made a month ago. Mike, a couple of years younger than Birdie, had left his job in Alberta and moved back into his mother's home for the time being. "There are no Canadian taxes on an inheritance," he said sounding a little relieved, "but I'm not sure about

Scottish law." He picked up the drink Birdie handed him, "and as the estate was considered my principle residence I don't think capital gains will come into it."

The two sat companionably in the library. A rectangular table with its corners cut off snuggled between their chairs. It was a dark table with brass inlays across the top. Birdie had had a glass covering made to protect the surface. "Let's let Jacob Bean worry about all the details, shall we? If there's tax to pay either way he will let me know"

He reached into his pocket and pulled out a cheque. "We've had two real estate companies provide us with an estimate of the estate's worth, nine hundred thirty pounds was the highest." He handed the cheque to Mike, "One million, nine hundred thousand dollars should cover it." Birdie could see Mike's hand shake a little as he took the cheque. He had wanted to remain in Canada to raise his family and Birdie was glad it worked out this way. Mike had an ancestry now he hadn't known before and now he would have money enough to see his family well taken care of. He would continue working he had said and save as much as he could for the future. He would fix up his mothers house and possibly add an extension for themselves. Mike was not a man given to extravagance Birdie had noted. Mike and his wife

Danielle had worked hard for the past few years and knew well the value of a dollar and with Victoria guiding him he wouldn't become the wastrel his Great, Great Uncle had become.

"Thank you, Cousin."

Once Birdie had seen the manor house with Kate he knew too where he wanted to raise his family. Kate had no qualms about leaving her past behind and decided she could write anywhere and that anywhere was here with Birdie.

"We have a meeting with Jacob tomorrow, but for now, let's join the others and enjoy the day."

Kate and Birdie had met with Alex Cheyne just once before taking over Cheyne Manor. He had been upset at first suddenly realizing he would have to raise money now on his own merit and that he would never be able to enjoy the life style he had been accustomed to all his life.

Duncan Cheyne on the other hand was an invalid and still alive needing more care than Alex could or would offer. Kate and Birdie had discussed Duncan with Mike and their lawyer Mr. Bean, and together had decided to allow a small yearly income to be set aside for Duncan's care in a private nursing home. They had no such charity for Alex though, who would have to find his own means of support.

The rest of the day was spent in touring the

grounds of the estate. The groundskeeper had been delighted with the task of explaining the estate history and all of its unique attributes. Kelly was especially interested in the horse stable while the men gravitated to the trout pond which was fed by a fresh creek that ran off the river Lyon a few miles away. Mike Lyonne had thought the name of the river very appropriate, considering the circumstances. Kate, Danielle and little Meg spent time in the flower garden with the gentle Airedale Bruce, who didn't seem to object to the little girl sitting on his back.

"You don't know how much this means to me," she confessed to Kate. "I'm so glad you were able to buy the property," then she looked at the little girl she held in her arms as Meg played horsey, "I could never leave my family back home."

"I know," said Kate and she took Meg off the large dog and held her in her arms, "I felt that way too for a while, but my place is with him." She nodded toward Birdie who had returned with the other men from their walk. "Besides, we can visit each other." She smiled when she saw Kelly sitting on a black mare that Cam now led slowly around the paddock adjoining the stables. He handed her the reins and let her take the horse a few laps on her own. She laughed, "Now that Kelly has discovered the horses I'm sure we'll be seeing more of her."

It was a week of sight seeing and shopping during the day and in the evening Birdie informed his new family of their heritage. He read passages from William's journal carefully excluding certain references and shared the pictures they had found. Birdie gave Mike his Grandfather's medals, carefully framed, and copies of the letters sent by Jean. Kelly and Ted were bound for London for another week of touring while Mike and Danielle were to take the train south to Birdie's parent's home near Oxford to meet Hannah.

Kate was in their bedroom when she heard the truck arrive, a delivery truck. Curious to see what had been delivered she ran down stairs to the main entrance. Mrs. Walker was signing for the box, a large box, as she reached the door. Birdie came through the kitchen having been helping the groundskeeper clear some fallen trees from the wooded area. His hands and face were dirty and he looked like one of the stable hands in his working clothes. "It's arrived!" he seemed genuinely surprised at the sight of the cardboard box. "I didn't think it would be ready until next week." Mrs. Walker had discretely left the two as Kate fingered the taped folds of the mysterious box.

"What is it?"

"Something for a special lady." he said

mysteriously.

Curious now Kate started to loosen the tape that held the flaps together. “Shall I?” offered Birdie. He took out the pen knife he always carried and slit the tape very carefully at the edges then ripped it off quickly across the top of the box. He opened up the flaps for Kate to get a better look.

“Oh, Birdie, it’s wonderful!” Kate ran her fingers slowly over the table top with the brass cat inlays identical to the ones in their original puzzle table.

“It’s not a puzzle table but I think she’ll like it,”

“I know she will,” said Kate.

# CONNOR CHEYNE FAMILY TREE

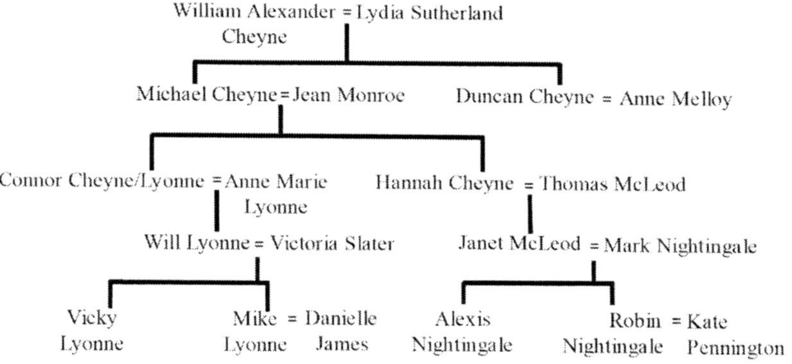

**Jacqueline Opresnik lives in Ontario, Canada, with her husband Frank and Bengal cat Tiggy. She received her degree in mathematics and geology from Brock University. She earned her pilot's license shortly after, where she met her husband. Jackie pursued a teaching career after completing teachers college. She has had a love of writing since she was ten and is just now beginning to fulfill her dreams as an author.**

CPSIA information can be obtained
at www.ICGtesting.com
Printed in the USA
LVOW12s1109291117
557952LV00001B/1/P